Fight or Flight?

FIGHT OR FLIGHT?
Mastering problems of everyday life

BEATRIX HUGHES MB, ChB and
RODNEY BOOTHROYD BA

faber and faber
LONDON · BOSTON

First published in 1985
by Faber and Faber Limited
3 Queen Square, London WC1N 3AU

Filmset by
Wilmaset, Birkenhead, Merseyside
Printed in Great Britain by
Whitstable Litho Ltd, Whitstable, Kent

All rights reserved

© Beatrix Hughes and Rodney Boothroyd 1985

This book is sold subject to the condition that it shall not, by way of trade or otherwise, be lent, resold, hired out or otherwise circulated without the publisher's prior consent in any form of binding or cover other than that in which it is published and without a similar condition including this condition being imposed on the subsequent purchaser

British Library Cataloguing in Publication Data

Hughes, Beatrix
Fight or flight: mastering problems of
everyday life
1. Health
I. Title II. Boothroyd, Rodney
613   RA776
ISBN 0-571-13591-9

Library of Congress Cataloging in Publication Data

Hughes, Beatrix.
Fight or flight?
1. Stress (Psychology)—Prevention. 2. Autogenic training. I. Boothroyd, Rodney. II. Title.
BF575.S75H83 1985   158'.1   85-1613
ISBN 0-571-13591-9 (pbk.)

Contents

	Acknowledgements	*page* 8
	Glossary	9
	Introduction	13
1	The Cause and Effects of Stress	15
2	How to Reduce Your Level of Stress	35
3	Stress and Relaxation	47
4	Hypnosis, Self-Hypnosis and the Tape Recorder Technique	57
5	Understanding Your Feelings and Emotions	74
6	Defeating Depression	79
7	What is Anxiety?	96
8	How to Control Your Anxiety	104
9	Fears and Phobias	117
10	Worried Thinking	136
11	Understanding Social Anxiety	145
	Further Reading	163
	Useful Addresses	165
	Index	169

Acknowledgements

Figure 5/1, page 76, is reproduced from *Fact and Fiction in Psychology* by permission of the publishers, Penguin Books Limited, London.

Table 1/1, page 17, is reproduced from *Stress* by Tom Cox, by permission of the publishers, Macmillan, London and Basingstoke.

The extract on pages 91–2 from *The Secret Strength of Depression* is reproduced by permission of the author, Fredric F. Flach, and the publishers, Angus and Robertson (UK) Limited, London W1R 4BN.

The extract on page 136 from *Stress, Sanity and Survival* is reproduced by permission of the authors, R. L. Woolfolk and F. C. Richardson, and the publishers, Macdonald and Co (Publishers) Limited, London EC2A 2EN.

The authors express their thanks to all the authors and publishers for these permissions.

Glossary

adrenalin A hormone secreted by the adrenal glands which affects circulation and muscle action

anxiety A feeling of apprehension, uncertainty and fear without apparent cause, which is associated with physiological changes such as palpitations, sweating, muscle tremor and so forth

arousal The state induced by the release of adrenalin. *Physical* arousal involves greater muscle tension and other bodily changes. *Mental* arousal involves an increased level of mental activity and greater alertness; at high levels of arousal, mental activity tends to become confused

autonomic nervous system That part of the nervous system which regulates the functions of some of the internal organs not normally under conscious control. It consists of two main divisions: the *sympathetic*, which increases arousal and action; and the *parasympathetic*, a division generally antagonistic to the sympathetic, which inhibits the action of the heart and augments intestinal action

autosuggestion A type of self-hypnosis. As the name suggests, one makes therapeutic suggestions to oneself, during a state of relaxation, and these pass into the subconscious mind

behavioural psychology The branch of psychology which aims to treat emotional problems, especially phobias, by concentrating on behavioural change and not on the analysis of repressed material

conditioning A process in which the subconscious mind learns to associate some particular stimulus with a particular response. In the case of phobias, the stimulus may be an object or place, for example, and the response is one of anxiety

coping behaviour This term includes any form of behaviour by which a person tries to lessen the effect of stress

corticoids A group of steroids produced by the cortex of the adrenal gland. Their production is greatly increased under conditions of major stress

counselling A form of psychotherapy which is aimed at providing someone who has emotional problems with a clearer understanding of, and insight into, their overall situation

defence mechanism This term includes any psychological processes by which a person tries to lessen the impact of stress on his or her mind and body. The most common defence mechanism is probably repression

depression An emotional state which involves feelings of sadness or unhappiness together with a lowering of self-esteem

depressive illness A form of depression of organic or emotional origin and not caused by some external situation

desensitisation A process of gradual exposure to a feared stimulus, with the aim of weakening the conditioned link between the stimulus and the anxiety response

fear The name generally applied to intense anxiety responses

fight or flight response Common name for the body's response to stressful situations. This response is controlled by the autonomic nervous system and involves increased physical and mental arousal. If sustained over a period of time, the fight or flight response can produce a wide variety of physical and emotional problems

generalisation A spontaneous process whereby a person's fears spread from a particular stimulus onto other ones of a similar nature

hormone A chemical substance produced in the body by the endocrine glands or cells of organs which has a specific regulatory effect on the activity of organs

hypnosis A process in which the activity of the conscious mind is reduced, thereby allowing information to pass directly into the subconscious

implosion A technique sometimes used to treat phobias, in which the phobic person visualises the object of his or her fear until the resulting anxiety declines in intensity

GLOSSARY

manic-depressive illness A mental disorder with severe mood swings from excessive elation and over-activity to a severely depressed state of mind

neurosis A mental or emotional disturbance in which there is no serious disturbance of the personality. Caused mainly by unresolved conflicts and anxiety

phobia An intense, irrational anxiety reaction to a stimulus which presents little or no objective danger

psychosis Mental disorder of organic or emotional origin characterised by the derangement of personality

psychosomatic disorder Body symptoms of mental or emotional origin

reactive depression A form of depression caused by some stressful situation. It is generally relieved when the situation is terminated

repression A defence mechanism which involves the suppression of stressful thoughts, feelings and emotions from the conscious to the subconscious mind

self-esteem A person's sense of self-worth; of value as an individual

self-hypnosis A technique in which the hypnotic state is self-induced

self-image The way one sees oneself, rightly or wrongly

stress The response in a person's body or mind when he or she perceives some threat to his or her emotional or physical well-being

visualisation The process of forming vivid mental images, usually with one's eyes closed. Can be used as a form of autosuggestion

Introduction

Stress is perhaps the most widespread social problem of our time for it can affect everyone, regardless of age, sex or occupation. This fact is reflected in the large number of books on the subject: a number so large, indeed, that one ought to have a good reason for adding to it. Our reason, simply, is that we feel we have something original and valuable to say. The basic aim of this book is to help people help themselves: Firstly, to obtain a clearer understanding of what stress is, what it can do to their minds and bodies, and how to identify it; and, secondly, both to reduce the amount of stress they experience and also to master the physical and emotional problems it can produce. To do this, we have adopted a two-fold approach.

The first line of attack is to show how one can identify and challenge the beliefs and assumptions about life which are responsible, directly or indirectly, for producing personal stress. The second line of attack is to describe how one can treat the symptoms of stress, particularly emotional problems, with simple self-help techniques. Although these techniques vary with the different emotions discussed, two key features of the book as a whole are relaxation and self-hypnosis. Relaxation and self-hypnosis are not new, of course, but our approach probably is. Above all, we have tried to ensure that the 'treatments' we describe are simple but *effective*.

One group of people who should find this book especially useful are those individuals who know they have some emotional trouble – be it anxiety, depression, a phobia, or whatever – and wish to deal with it themselves. Working on one's own can be like stumbling around in a darkened room; we hope to provide some light in the darkness. In addition, we would wish to express the hope that those in the healing profession, to whom patients turn for help, will obtain a little more understanding of how to guide their patients in coping with stress.

Finally, our thanks are due to all those who helped in preparing this book, but particularly to those researchers on stress whose ideas we have made use of, and to the people whose experiences we have described in the text.

BEATRIX HUGHES
RODNEY BOOTHROYD
1985

1. The Cause and Effects of Stress

We all experience stress; we cannot avoid it. Because of this daily contact with stress, we all have a vague idea of what it is and what it can do to our physical and mental health. But if you were asked to define stress, what would you say? Mental strain caused by the demands of life and work? That would be a typical answer, but it does not reveal why a stressed executive develops an ulcer, nor does it explain why stress causes depression in one man and an ulcer or heart attack in another, nor does it suggest that stress can be a result of either boredom and inactivity or overwork. Obviously a comprehensive definition of stress will set the scene for a better understanding of the problem. This is it:

> Stress is the reaction in an individual's body or mind when that person perceives a potential threat to his emotional or physical well-being.

This definition may not be elegant, but it is accurate. Psychologists now acknowledge that an event or situation is only stressful if you perceive it (that is, interpret it in your mind) as threatening. For example, if you were confronted in a dark street late at night by a man obviously intent on robbing you, your reaction would depend on how well you believed you could cope. If you were confident of your ability to defend yourself, you would remain much calmer than someone who expected to lose a fight.

That is an obvious example of a situation which involves the possibility of physical harm. However, as our definition of stress makes clear, the same principle applies to any experience which might affect your emotional well-being (i.e. your happiness, sense of security, self-esteem and so forth). Thus, for example, being criticised by someone is particularly stressful if you depend on that person's approval to maintain your own self-esteem. Similarly, the break-up of a relationship is far more stressful when your emotional security depends on the relationship than when you are emotionally self-reliant.

Thus there is no situation which, in itself, is stressful; even very dangerous situations only evoke a reaction if a person sees them as potentially harmful. You can see that this is true if you consider a young child playing on the edge of a busy road. Although he is in grave danger, he may well be quite unaware of the fact, probably feels quite happy, and only when he has been taught that roads and cars are dangerous will he perceive the threat to himself and react in some way.

This view of stress emphasises that a stress response is made up of different parts: the event, situation or environment in which a person finds himself; his appraisal of whether it is threatening or potentially harmful; and, lastly, his physical or emotional reaction to it. This reaction may be either a conscious action – such as leaving the stress situation – or a subconsciously controlled reaction like those listed in Table 1/1. (The conscious part of your mind is the part with which you think and observe the world; it is made up of everything in your mind of which you are aware while awake. The subconscious, by contrast, is outside conscious awareness, but nevertheless works 24 hours a day to control memory, thinking and sensory processes, and basic body systems such as breathing and digestion.)

Since a person's appraisal of a situation also involves subconscious as well as conscious processes, he or she may experience the symptoms of stress without knowing why. We shall discuss this in detail later in the chapter, but a simple example at this point will illustrate the idea. Consider a man who is stressed by his job but does not consciously realise that this is the cause of, say, his irritability. The problem may have begun with a conscious thought ('I hate this job!') which was then suppressed because it was unacceptable ('But I can't leave it because my family needs the security of my employment'). However, suppression of a thought from the conscious mind does not make it go away: it remains in the subconscious and produces a stress reaction of one sort or another.

Table 1/1 The effects and cost of stress (Cox, 1978)

---

1 Subjective effects
Anxiety, aggression, apathy, boredom, depression, fatigue, frustration, guilt and shame, irritability and bad temper, moodiness, low self-esteem, threat and tension, nervousness, and loneliness.

2 Behavioural effects
Accident proneness, drug taking, emotional outbursts, excessive eating or loss of appetite, excessive drinking and smoking, excitability, impulsive behaviour, impaired speech, nervous laughter, restlessness, and trembling.

3 Cognitive effects
Inability to make decisions and concentrate, frequent forgetfulness, hypersensitivity to criticism, and mental blocks.

4 Physiological effects
Increased blood and urine catecholamines and corticosteroids, increased blood glucose levels, increased heart rate and blood pressure, dryness of mouth, sweating, dilation of pupils, difficulty breathing, hot and cold spells, 'a lump in the throat', numbness and tingling in part of the limbs.

5 Health effects
Asthma, amenorrhoea, chest and back pains, coronary heart disease, diarrhoea, faintness and dizziness, dyspepsia, frequent urination, headaches and migraine, neuroses, nightmares, insomnia, psychoses, psychosomatic disorder, diabetes mellitus, skin rash, ulcers, loss of sexual interest, and weakness.

6 Organisational effects
Absenteeism, poor industrial relations and poor productivity, high accident and poor labour turnover rates, poor organisational climate, antagonism at work, and job dissatisfaction.

Perhaps surprisingly, a common mechanism lies behind all the different effects of stress shown in Table 1/1. We shall look at this mechanism before considering why different people show a variety of physical and emotional symptoms of stress.

THE MECHANISM OF STRESS

In dangerous situations which may require a greater than normal level of physical activity (such as fighting or running away from an enemy), many animals, including man, display the 'fight or flight' response. This is a bodily reaction which produces greater readiness for physical exertion; it is controlled by the sympathetic branch of the autonomic (meaning self-regulating) nervous system.

One of the functions of the sympathetic nervous system (SNS) is to control the release of the hormone adrenalin, which in turn raises the level of tension in the muscles of the body so that they are prepared for greater physical exertion. It also makes the heart pump faster and more deeply, thus producing that uncomfortable awareness of one's heart pounding away like a hammer in one's chest. Besides these physical effects, adrenalin also stimulates our feelings of fear, anger and exhilaration.

Other obvious bodily changes controlled by the SNS include: changes in the tension of the bowel and bladder sphincter muscles, diversion of blood from the skin and internal organs to the skeletal muscles (thus producing a pale face and a dry mouth), the halting of activity in the stomach and gut (producing 'butterflies' and that sinking feeling), and an increase in sweating as preparation to cool the body after any violent activity. There are other, more subtle changes, too. For example, one's pupils dilate, and the walls of one's blood vessels constrict, thereby increasing blood pressure.

The other branch of the autonomic nervous system – the parasympathetic – opposes all these changes. It has been called the 'rest-digest' system because it reduces muscle tension, stores energy and encourages digestion.

The evolution of the fight-flight response allowed animals to react automatically to danger. The need for humans to prepare for a fight to the death or rapid escape mostly disappeared as we became more civilised, though even now the fight-flight response is still evoked when we are in danger. And, of course, this is fine – if you do happen to need physical activity. Problems arise, however, because evolution has provided us with a thinking, conscious brain which allows us to perceive threats to our emotional well-being as well as threats of physical harm. In either case the result is the same: the subconscious switches on the fight-flight response. Thus, for example, we sit through an examination or interview with a pounding heart, a tense body, an upset stomach, unable to think clearly and generally very aroused. (Arousal refers to the effects of a general increase in activity of the SNS, including the release of adrenalin and associated increase in mental activity.)

While mild arousal may pass almost unnoticed and slightly greater arousal may actually improve one's performance, higher levels of arousal are a major factor in various forms of anxiety. We shall look at these problems in more detail in a later chapter, but at the moment we are more concerned with the effects of a mild but persistent level of arousal. The kind of situation which raises adrenalin levels is very common in our society and our lives: a man under pressure at work, a woman at home bringing up the family under financial constraints, a couple trapped in an unhappy marriage – all these people and many more will habitually experience mild but persistent levels of arousal.

THE PHYSICAL EFFECTS OF STRESS

The physical signs of increased arousal are: a tight throat, tension in the neck and back with the shoulders raised, shallow breathing, a rapid heart beat, a tight anus, cool but mildly perspiring hands and feet, tight leg muscles, clenched fists, a frowning face. Therefore, on a purely physical level, one sign of excessive stress is tension in the body muscles. Someone who claims to be suffering from 'nervous tension' is probably suffering a predominantly physical stress syndrome.

Prolonged and unabated stress can produce the wide variety of symptoms listed in Table 1/1. One of the most important of these is high blood pressure, or hypertension, which develops when adrenalin is released by the adrenal glands under conditions of stress. This causes the walls of the blood vessels to constrict, which in turn raises the blood pressure; and if the stress is frequently repeated or prolonged, may lead to a permanent state of high blood pressure.

Hypertension is very common in modern Western society and presents a serious medical problem because it is directly related to the high incidence of stroke, heart disease, arteriosclerosis and kidney failure. The connection with stress is undisputed. For example, air traffic controllers have one of the most stressful jobs possible, with continual responsibility for the lives of thousands of people; they also show levels of hypertension five times higher than the rest of the population.

Chronic stress produces a further change in body chemistry over and above the adrenalin release of the fight-flight response: the adrenal glands also begin to produce corticoid hormones in greater than normal quantities. The liver normally monitors the level of corticoids in the body, but during periods of prolonged stress, the liver's control system is by-passed and high levels of corticoids continue to flow around the body. Research has shown that this can lead to a loss of resistance to disease (a fact which most of us can confirm from our own experience, since, when we are under stress, we do seem more vulnerable to minor infections such as coughs and colds). Corticoids also seem to increase the resistance of body tissue to adrenalin. However, adrenalin production does not stop, and a 'battle' between the hormones develops, until eventually the excess adrenalin breaks through the corticoid screen at the weakest point in a person's body. This often takes the form of a stomach ulcer, because adrenalin increases the output of stomach acid, which then begins to attack the tissue of the stomach itself.

The noted expert on stress Hans Selye put forward some suggestions to explain why different people succumb to stress at different places in the body. We can understand this by considering the stressful effects of our environment such as extremes of heat and cold. These can be regarded as a form of stress because they are potentially dangerous and may lead to body damage. And in fact extremes of temperature do cause the production of adrenalin and corticoids. But in addition they also produce a specific effect: heat, for example, produces sweating and a flushed skin, while cold produces shivering and erection of body hair. When you realise that all stressful situations evoke their own specific response in the body as well as the non- specific adrenalin and corticoid reaction, you can begin to understand why the response of different individuals to stress is never exactly the same.

But this alone does not account for the extreme variability of physical stress symptoms between individuals. Consider the range of possibilities: heart disease, ulcers, constipation, diarrhoea, backache, asthma, dermatitis, colitis and rheumatism. And the list continues to increase, for recent research indicates that diabetes mellitus may be precipitated by stress and that the rate of recovery from cancer be slowed down considerably if stress is high. Hans Selye ascribes the variation in physical response to stress to heredity, environment, general health and fitness, behaviour and past illness. This is borne out by some simple observations. For example, if you have a genetic tendency to produce high levels of stomach acid, stress will probably cause an ulcer rather than heart disease. By contrast, a man on a high fat diet who also smokes heavily may find that stress affects his circulation and heart. This is because adrenalin causes a release of fat from body food stores; if the fat is not used for energy, it is not laid down again, but instead remains in the circulation and may be deposited on the walls of the arteries causing arteriosclerosis and coronary heart disease. Obviously if you consume a great deal of fatty food, the risk is much greater.

The influence of one's environment on stress-related disease shows up in various ways. Suppose that you watched your parents complaining about their tension headaches when you were a child. If you later experience stress in adulthood, is it not reasonable to suppose that you may develop tension headaches? Cultural factors also undoubtedly play a part in stress-related problems. Many people under stress report that they experience chest pains and think they are about to have a heart attack. This pain is caused by tension in the chest wall; it is very common and bears no relation to the heart. No doubt the reason why the problem is so common is our greater national awareness of heart disease because of extensive health-education campaigns. Finally, past illness can predispose certain parts of the body to break down under stress – rheumatic fever in childhood may make heart problems more probable later in life, for example.

There is one final peculiarity of these physical effects which we should mention before looking at the emotional side of stress. A person in stressful employment (such as long-distance lorry driving, hospital work and air traffic control) may work for years without any apparent ill-effects. He or she may then suddenly develop, let us say, stomach pains which are mild at first but soon become a full-blown ulcer. The person denies he is stressed because he has never before noticed any emotional or physical strain. This can happen because the level at which adrenalin and corticoids go on working during prolonged stress is below conscious awareness. Nevertheless, the damage continues inside the body, until eventually it becomes obvious as a stroke, heart attack, ulcer or some other serious disease. This is especially true when stress produces hypertension, which is often discovered only during routine blood pressure checks.

EMOTIONAL ASPECTS OF STRESS

We need to consider both emotionally induced stress and the emotional effects of stress.

EMOTIONALLY INDUCED STRESS

Stress can result from overwork; it can also result from boredom. This paradoxical nature of stress has been summed up by Dr Peter Tyrer. He relates an example of a man suffering from stress induced by employment in a job which is neither dangerous nor difficult, but simply boring: it consists of adding up rows of figures in the accounts section of a tax office. The man who is doing this job is emotionally unsuited to such dreary, routine work. He craves excitement and adventure – in fact, he finds the work so oppressive and boring that he is under considerable stress. This appears as strange impulses to falsify the figures on the accounts sheet with which he is working. Eventually he resents the tyranny of boredom so much that he leaves the job and goes to sea.

In this case the man's stress resulted from an emotional conflict between his need to enjoy his life and work (with some excitement and possibly danger) and his need to earn a wage in a secure job. Conflicts like this can be made worse by particular external pressures: if the man in the example above had been married, the need to behave responsibly for his wife and children's security would have increased the pressure on him to stay in the job where he was so unfulfilled. Clearly, then, stress is not only a problem for the highly pressured businessman with a great deal of responsibility; it is, in fact, just as likely to affect the discontented housewife living a life of boring routine, or the unemployed teenager who feels rejected by society, or anyone with a persistent source of unhappiness in their life – and, no doubt, many other types of people as well.

THE EMOTIONAL EXPERIENCE OF STRESS

The fact that stress is an emotional experience has been recognised in our society by the way in which stressed people talk about their condition. They do not say 'I am stressed' but: 'I am anxious/depressed/fearful/angry.' Stress can produce as many different emotions as it can physical effects, although the situation is complicated by the fact that an emotion may be a result of, or a causative factor in, stress. And once an emotion has developed, it may cause further stress.

Two of the most common emotional effects of stress are anxiety and depression. Chapters 6 and 7 will examine the ways in which these emotions develop, explain how they affect people, and consider what can be done about them.

An especially important point is the different roles which the conscious and subconscious play in human emotions. Our conscious perceptions cause stress, and thereby produce emotional problems. Changing one's perceptions about the world can therefore help to control emotional problems. However, that in itself is not usually sufficient, because patterns of emotional responses and behaviour may become firmly fixed in the subconscious mind so that they are no longer open to reasoning and conscious effort. Some techniques that *are* useful in dealing with them are discussed in Chapters 3 and 4.

THE WAYS IN WHICH WE ESCAPE STRESS

Stress can produce highly unpleasant physical and emotional symptoms, so it is therefore no surprise that people show various behaviour patterns designed to lessen its effects. These behaviour patterns are termed 'coping behaviour'. Coping behaviour is really a form of problem solving where the object is to safeguard one's own well-being but one is not quite certain how to do so. The two main types of coping behaviour are 'direct action' and 'palliative'.

Direct action tends to be dramatic, unthinking and automatic. Although it provides relief from stress in the short term, its long-term effects may be deleterious. For example, men or women under intolerable stress may decide to escape from their environment. At any university, most tutors would be able to offer at least one case where an apparently successful student arrived on his tutor's doorstep one morning just before the exams with the announcement that he has decided to defer sitting them, either for one year or permanently. A more dramatic gesture would be to walk out in the middle of an exam paper. The principle is clear: *direct* action involves physical or psychological action designed to remove or lessen stress, by making a rational (or irrational) effort to alter one's environment or circumstances.

Palliation behaviour can also take a number of forms. Each one of us will recognise at least one of these behavioural attempts to escape stress. Firstly, there is the use of alcohol, tranquillisers or relaxation techniques, which are symptom-directed techniques, in that they are aimed at the physical and emotional effects of stress rather than its cause. Secondly, there are intellectual defence mechanisms of the type described by Freud, which enable an individual to disguise the existence of a real or imagined threat from himself. The most important of these are: displacement, repression, denial, rationalisation, intellectualisation and reaction formation.

Displacement simply means the redirection of activity into a different form. It is not a redirection of stress itself, but a redirection of direct coping activity in situations where the coping behaviour is redirected and expressed as aggression, anger or sex. In the latter case, excessive masturbation or intercourse frequently hides the fact that a person is stressed and either unwilling or unable to alleviate the problem by direct coping behaviour. Sexual displacement is probably irrelevant to high levels of stress, but undoubtedly alleviates mild, persistent stress. There is a sound biological reason why a person comes to use sex as a method of reducing stress: the early stages of sexual activity are controlled by the parasympathetic nervous system, which, as you may recall, opposes the action of the sympathetic system. (Because digestion is controlled by the parasympathetic, eating a good meal may also alleviate the effects of stress.)

Repression means exactly what it implies: the suppression of stressful thoughts, perceptions and emotions from the conscious to the subconscious. Repression is unquestionably the most harmful palliative behaviour pattern because it can lead to severe depression and anxiety. This often happens when a man dies, leaving his widow alone after many years of marriage. Although her friends and relatives may say how well she seems to have got over the bereavement, and how quickly she has adjusted, in reality the stress and emotional impact of the death is being repressed. It may even be that the shock was of such magnitude that the woman felt no emotion at the time – this is not uncommon – and she went on living an apparently normal life. The stress, however, continues to build up until it finally erupts as a deep depression some months later. There are many similar situations where a person who has experienced an enormously traumatic event may carry on to all appearances quite normally, while the stress builds up in the subconscious mind.

Repression is actually very common. For example, you may accidentally 'forget' an appointment or invitation that causes you great anxiety, or you may repress memories of an incident which caused you great embarrassment so that they cannot be consciously recalled and so evoke further emotional discomfort. But whatever their cause, repressed thoughts, feelings and emotions do not just 'go away': they are retained in the subconscious, which is still affected by them. As we shall see, repression can cause anxiety, depression, phobias and worry.

Denial is a term which refers to psychological self-deceit. The student who is terrified by the prospect of his exams may neither decide to postpone them nor walk out in the middle; he may simply deny that they are of any relevance or importance to his future career, and that it will not matter if he fails them.

Rationalisation involves reasoning out logically acceptable but false explanations for certain events. For example, suppose that an individual is competing for a greatly desired promotion at work. If he fails to get it, he may reduce his feelings of disappointment and failure by rationalising that his employers were unfairly biased in favour of the other candidate or prejudiced against him. He may even convince himself that he 'did not want the job anyway'. Thus he accepts an interpretation of the situation which means he does not have to admit that he simply was not good enough for the job.

Intellectualisation is a process which operates in many situations where potentially enormous stress exists. A doctor who sees an endless succession of seriously ill patients may come to regard each person as an intellectual exercise in diagnosis rather than a 'real' man or woman. Intellectualisation thus involves emotional detachment – in effect, a 'switching-off' of our emotions, so that we cannot feel the effects of the stress under which we are working or living.

Reaction formation starts with the repression of unacceptable thoughts, feelings and emotions which are then replaced by exaggerated versions of their opposites. For example, a man who lacks confidence tries to be the 'life and soul of the party'; or a person with feelings of guilt about sexual activity (because he believes it to be 'dirty', say) develops an obsession about cleanliness.

THE BENEFITS OF STRESS

So far, we have been referring to stress in the sense of 'distress', but there are several ways in which stress can be beneficial or even enjoyable. First of all, dangerous situations or sports can be so uplifting and thrilling that adrenalin produces a sense of euphoria rather than danger. Similarly, joyous events may increase our arousal but our subjective impression is that they are highly enjoyable and well worth experiencing.

We can be fairly certain that stress can be beneficial by considering what happens when we are subjected to too little excitement and activity. During periods of dull monotony we become bored and the edge is removed from our intellectual and practical performance. Equally, many actors and performers require a good dose of adrenalin to arouse them sufficiently to add life and sparkle to their performances. Many examination candidates or people attending an interview are surprised to find that their increased arousal helps them to think more clearly and tackle the situation with far greater energy and determination than usual. But when one's level of arousal increases too much, it can be a hindrance rather than a help. When a person is over-aroused, he or she may feel nervous or frightened rather than excited, and, instead of performing well, may 'go to pieces'. Clearly the lesson of all this is that too little arousal is as bad as too much. Somewhere between there is an optimum – a point at which the adrenalin flows just fast enough to make the brain sharper and quicker and improve our performance when we need to be at our best. That is the good and beneficial side of stress.

WHEN STRESS BECOMES HARMFUL

There is no easy way to predict what sort of stress, or how much, will produce an individual's optimum level of arousal. Fortunately, it is easy to identify groups of people who, on the whole, are at risk from harmful stress. The most obvious one consists of people who are stressed in their employment, and it is this which we shall now examine.

Highly-pressured, ambitious businessmen are often regarded as very likely to suffer stress-related heart disease. One study conducted in 1958 by Russek and Zohman investigated the onset of heart attacks and angina in 100 male heart patients between the ages of 25 and 40. It was found that before their heart attacks, 91 per cent of the men had been subject to prolonged stress associated with the responsibility they had been expected to take in the course of their employment. A comparison with 100 men of similar age who did not have heart problems showed only 20 per cent who were under a great deal of stress. This does not prove that stress at work causes heart problems, but it is highly suggestive. In 1962 Russek provided more evidence for the connection between occupation and heart disease when he investigated occupation stress and the incidence of heart disease in doctors. He found that doctors in the more stressful roles such as general practice or anaesthetics had a level of heart disease almost four times greater than that of pathologists and dermatologists.

We must be careful not to forget that these investigations may simply have proved that heart disease is linked to particular personality traits such as enthusiasm and determination. These qualities could easily explain why people are given greater responsibility at work. The connection between personality and heart disease was investigated by Friedman (1974) who analysed the personalities of many heart patients and found that they showed a particular set of characteristics:

1. an intense sustained ambition to achieve self-selected but poorly defined goals
2. a greatly pronounced tendency and eagerness to compete
3. a persistent desire for recognition and advancement
4. a continuous involvement in many different job aspects all of which are up against time limits
5. a marked tendency to work more quickly than necessary, both physically and mentally
6. constant mental and physical alertness

If you recognise yourself in the above descriptions, it may be wise to take steps to reduce stress, although there are, of course, other factors involved in heart disease besides personality. To take just one example, the relationship between smoking, dietary fats, exercise and stress is not completely clear. But stress at work clearly predisposes some people to develop heart problems and actually making yourself aware of this could prevent a fatal attack.

You may wonder how the results of these investigations relate to our definition of stress (which indicates that an individual must perceive a potential threat to his physical and emotional well-being before he experiences stress). In fact it is not difficult to imagine a number of possible connections. For example, all the characteristics in the list above are traits of personality which would lead to someone taking responsibility very seriously. And a person who takes responsibility seriously is likely to be disturbed by the prospect of any failure. Responsibility also leads to worry which is a major cause of stress.

But there is, of course, more to it than that. Tom Cox and Colin Mackay have developed a theory to explain the origin of employment-related stress (Cox, 1978). They suggest that stress develops when somebody is subjected to internal and external demands which exceed his capability to meet those demands.

THE CAUSE AND EFFECTS OF STRESS

Internal demands take the form of one's own desire for a fulfilling job conducted in a reasonably comfortable environment with good working conditions and pay. Fulfilment may be interpreted individually; for example, work which presents a mental challenge or provides a particularly appreciated reward for success may be fulfilling for one person but not for another.

External demands are basically the psychological and physical requirements of an individual's employment. They are the sum total of such factors as the length of the working week, the periods of rest provided, the quality of work and the physical effort required. Nobody realised for many years that physical factors could be important in inducing stress; it is now understood that problems such as intense noise and repeatedly doing the same simple physical task produce stress and anxiety. One other demand which may be placed on somebody in their work is the need to play a role which is unsuited to their basic temperament and personality or the need to play two contradictory roles simultaneously. For example, a man who is asked to undertake some business which he regards as unethical or immoral will be in conflict between his own standards of behaviour and the role he is expected to play. Not unnaturally, if an individual's role is ill-defined, he is also likely to be stressed because he is unsure of his objectives, his colleagues' expectations, whom he should report to, and what his responsibilities consist of. Problems like this lead to 'tension, lack of fulfilment, sense of futility, reduced self-esteem and confidence', and these feelings must in turn cause even more stress. All in all, 30 million working days a year are lost through employment-related stress, not to mention the amount of job dissatisfaction which exists because of it.

Another major cause of stress is unhappiness in personal relationships. This often shows up as irritability, moodiness, aggression, anxiety and depression rather than in a more physical way. People who are under stress for reasons like this are often well aware of the cause of their stress but do not know how to deal with it. We shall offer some suggestions for changing the situation in Chapter 2.

As already mentioned, worry is a common cause of stress and increased arousal. This is because worried thinking actually involves the creation of perceptions of threat. (In other words, one spends time and energy imagining all the possible ways in which things might go wrong, and the possible effects if things *do* go wrong.) Such thoughts can trigger the body's stress response system as effectively as objectively real threats. Chapter 10 is devoted to certain aspects of the habit of worried thinking.

RECOGNISING HARMFUL STRESS

Stress is generally not harmful over a few days or even a few weeks, as long as it is not intense. But when it is prolonged over a period of months or years it will be harmful in one way or another: if it does not produce some physical effect, it may well lower your efficiency to a point where effective coping with life and work is no longer possible. Additionally, stress lowers your resistance to psychological trauma and physical illness, besides simply making you feel wretched. So how can you tell whether or not you are stressed? There are, in fact, several methods. Some rely on simple self-observation; others are slightly more sophisticated and involve some system of measurement. Let us consider first of all the simpler methods of self-observation. We can list these as follows:

PHYSICAL AND EMOTIONAL SYMPTOMS

Stress shows up either as physical or emotional symptoms, or both. You can therefore use Table 1/1, page 17, to check whether you have any overt symptoms of stress. Some particularly common symptoms are physical tension, poor sleep, a general emotional malaise or feeling of dissatisfaction with life, anxiety, irritability, and depression.

COPING BEHAVIOUR

It is possible to identify stress through some of the ways in which people try to deal with it. Some people respond to stress with frantic activity, aggression or drive in the belief that they are 'mastering' their situation and working very efficiently. In reality the way they throw themselves from activity to activity in a relentless effort to leave the stress behind simply causes further psychological strain. Others try to lessen the effects of stress with tranquillisers or alcohol, or indeed any of the other coping behaviours listed earlier (pp. 24–6).

THE QUALITY OF PERSONAL RELATIONSHIPS

The best clue may be the people around you. If the atmosphere in your family seems to have changed, or your friends seem to shun your company, or your employees remark on the fact that you used to be a much more reasonable person, perhaps you should consider whether the problems lies with you, not them?

A DECREASE IN PERSONAL EFFICIENCY

Stress tends to reduce your ability to discriminate between the essential and the non-essential, so that you may become preoccupied with unimportant matters while major problems remain to be solved. This means you work more and more but achieve less and less. Stress can also adversely affect your mental and physical co-ordination and muscular skill.

LIFESTYLE

The fact that one's lifestyle can be a sign of stress may be obvious, but obvious points are often overlooked. Many people in society battle on against their stress-related problems without clearly recognising the situation they are in. For example, many of us will be able to think of at least one 'high-powered' man or woman: someone who takes on more and more work, never delegating responsibility for fear of 'the job not being done correctly'; always busy, often frenetic, showing signs of sleeplessness and increasing fatigue. And then there is the young housewife and mother, cooking meals, keeping house, coping with her children, who often seems 'at her wit's end'. In quite the reverse way, some people allow events and circumstances to determine their course through life, perhaps because they do not know how to control events or because they lack the confidence to stand up for themselves. Such a passive acceptance of events can be genuinely stressful and lead to resentment, loss of self-esteem and depression.

Nowadays, another common cause of stress is unemployment

with its attendant financial and social problems. Family life and home affairs, too, are all potential sources of stress. In this kind of situation, you should question whether the pressures on you really are an inevitable and necessary part of your life structure. We shall examine this point more fully in subsequent chapters.

PREDICTING THE CONSEQUENCES OF STRESS

Obviously the methods described above are more relevant when you are already stressed. By contrast, it is possible to *predict* whether recent events in one's life are likely to induce a stress-related illness. This idea was derived from research in 1967 by Thomas Holmes and Richard Rahe of the University of Washington, who questioned over 5000 people and found a high degree of correlation between the onset of stress-related illness and certain life events. Each of these events was then ascribed an LCU (Life Change Unit) value, which indicates the amount of stress it is potentially capable of producing. The full list is shown in Table 1/2. It is called the 'Social Readjustment Rating Scale', or SRRS for short.

Table 1/2. Social readjustment rating scale

Rank	Life event	Value
1	Death of spouse	100
2	Divorce	73
3	Marital separation	65
4	Jail term	63
5	Death of close family member	63
6	Personal injury or illness	53
7	Marriage	50
8	Fired at work	47
9	Marital reconciliation	45
10	Retirement	45
11	Change in health of family member	44
12	Pregnancy	40
13	Sex difficulties	39

Table 1/2. (*continued*)

Rank	Life event	Value
14	Gain of new family member	39
15	Business readjustment	39
16	Change of financial state	38
17	Death of close friend	37
18	Change to different line of work	36
19	Change in number of arguments with spouse	35
20	Mortgage over £10 000	31
21	Foreclosure of mortgage or loan	30
22	Change in responsibilities at work	29
23	Son or daughter leaving home	29
24	Trouble with in-laws	29
25	Outstanding personal achievement	28
26	Wife begins or stops work	26
27	Begin or end school	26
28	Change in living conditions	25
29	Revision of personal habits	24
30	Trouble with boss	23
31	Change in work hours or conditions	20
32	Change in residence	20
33	Change in schools	20
34	Change in recreation	19
35	Change in church activities	19
36	Change in social activities	18
37	Mortgage or loan less than £10 000	17
38	Change in sleeping habits	16
39	Change in number of family get-togethers	15
40	Change in eating habits	15
41	Vacation	13
42	Christmas	12
43	Minor violations of the law	11

Source: Holmes and Rahe (1967)

You can use the SRRS by adding up all the LCU values of the events which have happened to you *in the past year*. Then:

- A score of less than 150 means there is a 37% probability (3.7 in 10 chance) of your becoming ill in the next two years.

- A score between 150 and 300 means there is a 51% probability (5.1 in 10 chance) of your becoming ill in the next two years.
- A score over 300 means that there is an 80% probability (8 in 10 chance) of your becoming ill over the next two years.

We must emphasise certain points about the SRRS. First of all, if you obtain a score of, say, 320 you need not panic. The ratings were derived from an average American population between 1949 and 1967. Times have changed, and events which were very stressful at one time may no longer be so. Furthermore, the table is an average, and in all averages there are extremes. For example, retirement may be very boring and therefore unusually stressful for one person, but produce only 'average' stress in someone whose time is fully occupied. Secondly, more recent research has indicated that events may produce harmful stress only if we regard them as negative or unpleasant. But despite these notes of caution, the SRRS remains a useful *general* guide to your level of stress and the problems it can cause.

To recognise and admit that you are stressed may require careful self-analysis and total honesty. Consciously recognising that you are stressed means admitting that something in your environment disturbs you; and that implies change and effort to do something about it.

REFERENCES

Cox, T. (1978). *Stress*, p. 150. Macmillan, London.

Friedman, M. and Rosenman, R. H. (1974). *Type 'A' Behaviour and Your Heart*. Knopf, New York: Wildwood House, England.

Holmes, T. H. and Rahe, R. H. (1967). Social readjustment scale. *Journal of Psychosomatic Research*, **2**, 213.

Russek, H. I. and Zohman, B. L. (1958). Relative significance of heredity, diet and occupational stress in coronary heart disease of young adults. *American Journal of the Medical Sciences*, **235**, 266.

Russek, H. I. (1962). Emotional stress and coronary heart disease in American physicians, dentists and lawyers. *American Journal of the Medical Sciences*, **243**, 716.

2. How to Reduce Your Level of Stress

First of all, you must accept that stress is a personal problem rather than a medical one. Many people find it difficult to accept that they have the responsibility of helping themselves overcome stress and they go to their doctor looking for a magical cure which will 'relieve the tension'. But most family doctors cannot really be expected to do more than offer a prescription for a tranquilliser. This is because they simply do not have enough time to talk through emotional or psychological problems with all their patients, particularly if the background is rather complicated. Now, tranquillisers are effective and fast acting, but they do not remove the source of the stress. Rather like a man who drinks alcohol to relax, the man or woman who takes a tranquilliser may find it works very well at first, but that they are needed in ever-increasing doses as the body adapts to their action and becomes less responsive. When the tablets (or the alcohol) are stopped, the problems remain and may even seem worse. At best, tranquillisers are a means of reducing the physical or mental agony that severe stress can produce during a life crisis. Beyond that, each man and woman must be responsible for reducing the effects of stress on him or herself. This can be done either by changing your beliefs about your environment, your relationship to it and yourself, so that you no longer perceive situations as threatening, or by lessening the effects of stress through deep relaxation.

CHANGING YOUR BELIEFS ABOUT YOUR ENVIRONMENT AND YOURSELF

Ultimately, all harmful stress is caused by a perception of threat based on inappropriate, harmful, mistaken or unquestioned beliefs. For example: a man stressed in his job believes he has no option but to continue in that employment. A housewife living a life of drudgery believes she has no choice but to go on doing so. A highly nervous exam candidate believes that failure would be a personal disaster. A man unable to socialise freely believes that other people are likely to reject him. A less able schoolboy believes that he is the most stupid child ever born. A teenage girl believes she is unattractive. A man frightened to ask a woman for a date believes she may not like him and that rejection would be a catastrophe. And so on. It is this kind of belief which leads to perception of threat and so causes emotional arousal. Quite frequently, these beliefs are faulty or mistaken because they are based on wrong information or harmful past experience. Usually, they are accepted as fact without any questioning; they are mere assumptions. Changing these beliefs, or at least re-examining them, can alter our perceptions and so reduce stress. The process extends over every aspect of our lives. In this section, we are mostly concerned with beliefs which relate to our environment or life situation. We shall discuss the beliefs about oneself in Chapter 11 (social anxiety) because the subjects of social anxiety, beliefs about oneself, self-image and self-confidence are inextricably bound together. In this section, we shall examine beliefs about relationships, work, and life in general with specific attention on how they may be challenged and, when appropriate, changed for the better.

It is very common to see people who are so severely stressed at home or in their job that they are working at only a fraction of their real capacity and are racked by psychosomatic and emotional problems. Yet, if you ask them why they don't do something about the situation, they reply: 'Oh, I can't possibly change my job/move home/leave my wife.' This type of response may be merely a way of avoiding positive action which could change the situation. A fear of the unknown keeps many people within their existing environment, on the basis of 'better the devil you know, than the devil you don't.' On the other hand, such remarks can also be genuine but mistaken beliefs about oneself and the position one is in. 'I can't possibly change my job.' Why not? All one has to do is to sit down and examine the accuracy of each assumption which contributes to that overall

HOW TO REDUCE YOUR LEVEL OF STRESS

belief. As we shall see, this process is essentially one of strengthening your objective, reasoning, adult decision-making ability. You can grasp the principle involved from the following examples, which are intended to demonstrate the process of questioning your accepted beliefs and assumptions.

Firstly, let us consider John and Mary, a married couple who are constantly engaged in a struggle for power within their relationship. Constant arguments and conflict produce almost unbearable stress and great unhappiness. The options open to John and Mary are, however, very simple: either they separate or they stay together. If they choose the first option, they will have to decide whether or not to get a divorce. If they choose the second, they will either go on as they are or they will have to learn to live together more amicably. Let us suppose that they decide they would like a divorce, but are restrained from obtaining one by fear of their parents' disapproval. A professional counsellor might help them escape from this trap in the following way.

JOHN: We can't get a divorce, it's out of the question.
(This sounds like an assumption.)
COUNSELLOR: Why is it out of the question?
MARY: Because of the shame that it would bring on us.
(A faulty belief.)
COUNSELLOR: Why do you consider divorce is shameful? When one marriage in four ends in divorce, it must be socially acceptable.
JOHN: Our friends and parents wouldn't like it.
(Probably another assumption.)
COUNSELLOR: Don't you already know some divorced couples? What do you think about their divorce?
MARY: Yes, but I'm talking about what our parents would say.
COUNSELLOR: Why should you remain trapped in a miserable marriage just because of what you think your parents might say?
MARY: I know they wouldn't approve. After all, mine have been together for thirty years.
COUNSELLOR: How do you know they wouldn't approve? Have you asked them?
MARY: No.

COUNSELLOR: Who is running your life, anyway? You or your parents?
JOHN: Well, we are, I suppose.
COUNSELLOR: Who should make the decision about divorce?

Hopefully, the answer which either John or Mary now gives is: 'We should.' Human nature being what it is, they are more likely to say something like: 'Yes, but divorce isn't that simple. You have to think of other people.' The difficulty lies in getting them to see that ultimately no-one else should be able to exert control over their lives. They bear ultimate responsibility for changing matters; they make the rules for themselves.

As a whole, the process is designed to assist them to question the beliefs which they hold, so that eventually they gain enough insight into these faulty and unquestioned beliefs to allow them to establish new, autonomous views about life and their position in it. If they had decided that they preferred to stay together, they could have used a similar technique to improve their relationship.

As a second example, consider a man who is stressed by his job. Let us imagine that he is overworked and underpaid, never gets a word of thanks from his employers and has poor relationships with his colleagues because they abuse his willingness to take on extra work. When he wakes up each morning, his first thought is: 'I wish I didn't have to go today!' He works hard all day, meeting deadlines, working on several projects at once, perhaps even working over his lunch hour and taking work home. All his working life is pressured and stressed, which makes him unhappy and unfulfilled. He wants to leave the job but never does so – simply because he does not question his unstated assumption that he couldn't leave the job. If you were in this situation, there are various ways in which you might begin to challenge your assumptions. Here are a few examples:

'I can't leave my job because . . .
. . . I have no skills for anything else.'

But nobody suggested that you should abandon your current occupation. You could look for work in the same field with a different employer.

. . . this is a time of high unemployment.'

The ease with which you find another job does rather depend on how much demand there is for your special skills or abilities. Obviously, during periods of high unemployment, that demand may be lower. But there are still hundreds of thousands of people changing jobs every week. In any case, why couldn't you retrain in a different work field or take temporary work while looking for a new position?

. . . I won't be able to retrain.'

But why not? With enough determination you can do anything at any age. And there are areas of work where skilled people are in short supply. Alternatively, many people find great satisfaction in setting up their own business. There are plenty of opportunities for franchising, for example.

. . . I shall be short of money, and what about my family?'

Of course, responsibility extends to caring for one's family materially as well as emotionally. If you really would be short of money, why not sell the car, move to a smaller house, or make a real effort to find a new job before leaving your existing one?

Your first consideration in any such self-analysis should always be what will be best for you in the long term. Because the effects of stress can be so debilitating – even fatal – you might be better off without a car and a job but with your health intact. The process of questioning beliefs can be a lengthy one. ('Sell the car? How could we manage without one?' Well, do you really need a car? Why?) It is also a very personal process, and the results which you achieve will depend on how motivated you really are to avoid stress.

Sometimes, it has to be said, one goes through this process and decides that one's beliefs are correct. If a man finds he cannot give up a stressful job, say, because he believes that financial security is too important to relinquish, then nobody has the right to expect him to do so. In such a case, there is an effective alternative method of coping with stress: that is, reducing one's level of arousal by learning to relax, a technique which is explained in Chapter 3.

There are occasions when one's beliefs are correct (as far as anyone's can be) and a conflict between those beliefs and what one is doing seems to cause stress. Peter B. is a friend of ours who worked for many years with a company which sold pharmaceuticals and artificial baby foods to the Third World. Although the job was very well paid, he found it highly stressful, and he eventually developed an ulcer. This caused him to stop and question what he was doing for the first time in many years. He realised that he had been ignoring the fact that he had serious doubts about the ethics and morality of the profit-oriented business he was involved with. He told us how this insight had sparked off a session of self-analysis. 'First of all,' he recalled, 'I had to find out whether my doubts were objectively valid. I researched the opinions and statements of doctors, both in the West and in our sale areas. I spent some time looking at the comments of government ministers in the Asian and African countries to which we sold these high tech. products. I realised that poor people were spending a large proportion of their income on drugs and baby foods which were unnecessary but freely available. Uncontrolled by doctors, they were probably suffering rather than benefiting. There was no doubt in my mind that I wasn't just prejudiced. This was no irrational attitude; I couldn't go on ignoring my conscience any longer. I quit the job.'

In general terms there are comparatively few categories of belief that can lead to stress. Here are some of the more important ones.

1. *Believing that a highly competitive, win or lose, 'dog eat dog' situation exists in the world, and that every conflict of personalities or events must produce a winner and a loser.* Such a belief may lead to a loss of self-esteem and a great deal of stress even in objectively insignificant circumstances. If you lay your self-esteem on the line in every situation you enter, it is inevitable that you will become stressed.
2. *Believing that other people are basically untrustworthy or unpleasant, and expecting the worst from them in whatever you may be doing.* This is a form of prejudice based on ignorance or, sometimes, previously distressing interpersonal relationships. Such an attitude can only lead to a sense of bitterness, condemnation and intolerance of other men and women; these attitudes are highly stress-producing and harm only the person who holds them by removing any possibility of seeking

HOW TO REDUCE YOUR LEVEL OF STRESS

out and obtaining emotional fulfilment. The truly content man has no prejudice against his fellow humans. If you do find someone personally intolerable, the answer is to remove yourself from their presence.

3. *Believing that life can provide everything you want with no real effort on your part.* Such expectations are quite unreal and lead to frustration, lack of motivation and effort and an ultimate failure to achieve anything at all.

4. *Believing that problems can be resolved without action; in other words, tolerating a stress-producing situation and making no effort to change it.* In difficult circumstances, people do lose motivation, but there is always some answer to a problem – the difficulty may be finding it, and that is an individual task. This belief is of course very closely related to an attitude which is very common today, namely that an individual has no responsibility to solve his own problems because someone else will do it. This is one of the objections to the 'nanny state' where responsibility for individuals' well-being has passed into the hands of social workers, doctors and government agencies rather than resting where it primarily should – with the family and individual.

5. *Believing that other people should abide by your code of behaviour.* This kind of 'moralistic thinking' leads to indignation, frustration, aggression and a desire to punish or revenge. You have no reason to assume that your own code of behaviour has anything more than subjective value. If someone else breaks your code with an act which you find unacceptable, you should recall that they have acted in accordance with their own standards of behaviour. No doubt these are as valid to them as your standards are to you.

6. *Believing in meaningless objectives which are pressured on to you by the expectations of other people.* For example, a rosy image of life as ideally happy and fulfilled may lead people to feel guilty if they are unhappy! Equally, many people live by a code of values which rests on the belief that prosperity is a measure of success and is therefore highly desirable. Success itself may even become a person's highest aim. The problem with beliefs like this is that the goals they set are unattainable, because there is always one higher step which you could achieve – but which is actually held by somebody else.

Prosperity, success or progress are not ends in themselves, as some people believe; they should merely be means to an end – a fulfilled existence. The search for prosperity, success or progress as ends in themselves is perhaps one of the most stressful ways of life imaginable, if only because one constantly falls short of what is imagined to be the 'ideal' standard. The same applies to a search for happiness, since life inevitably produces some unhappy experiences – this is a normal part of the human condition.

7. *Believing that your value as a person must be judged by your ability to measure up to a set of standards imposed by other people.* This is a sure formula for stress. The same applies to the mistaken belief that you can evaluate your personal worth by evaluating what you do. There is a distinction between what you are and what you do. We shall return to this subject later.

8. *Believing that you are dependent on another person for your emotional security.* This is, of course, called 'dependency'. Emotionally close relationships are important for everyone, but it is risky to make your own sense of security dependent upon these relationships. People and relationships change and therefore stress develops very easily if a relationship actually controls a person's sense of self-worth. But even for those who are not dependent on another person, the ending of a relationship is still one of life's most stressful events. Robert Woolfolk and Frank Richardson (1979) believe that this is only partly attributable to our fear of losing the rewarding quality of a relationship. They suggest that many people fear loss because they believe, wrongly, that if they lose an important relationship they will be unable to find another person who is of equal value. Removing this source of stress really implies developing confidence in oneself and one's ability to establish relationships as and when necessary or desirable.

As should now be obvious, our whole existence is based on beliefs, some right, some wrong, and some dangerous. In the course of this book, we shall come across many other faulty beliefs which can cause stress. For example, many people believe that worry is productive and necessary, whereas it is actually futile and emotionally exhausting. Correcting faulty beliefs like that through the sort of critical thought and self-examination we suggest here will not only reduce your level of stress, but also remove one of the ultimate causes of physical and emotional problems.

This is not the place to try and discuss a philosophy of life. But it *is* important for everyone to have a personal philosophy – a set of beliefs, if you like – by which they can live. This might take the form of a willing tolerance of other people and their shortcomings, or the more positive attitude of 'Love Thy Neighbour as Thyself' – as Hans Selye puts it, 'Earn Thy Neighbour's Love.' Such philosophies do not exclude material success; rather, they provide a framework within which all achievements are possible. Below are some general suggestions on reducing the stress of your environment. They do not make a philosophy of life; they do no more than serve as some suggestions for the basis of your own actions.

GUIDELINES TOWARDS A LOWER-STRESS LIFESTYLE

1. Hans Selye maintains that we can only be fulfilled when we have an aim in life; that frustration and stress produced by indecision and uncertainty only cease to exist when we are following a path through life towards that aim; and that short-term goals for immediate gratification must be supplemented by long-term goals with measurable reward on the way to the ultimate aim. As examples of long-term objectives he mentions philosophical, religious and political ideals. (There are, of course, many more.) However, the pursuit of money or 'success' or 'happiness' is only a means to an end, not an end in itself. The choice of an aim and the means by which it can be achieved are a very personal matter.
2. The suppression of basic emotional desires is something which inevitably leads to stress and frustration. One example is the common belief that it is 'unmanly' for men to show the emotion which they feel. Another is our reluctance to admit that we crave approval and love and fear censure or ridicule. One should question carefully whether such accepted

standards of behaviour in our own social group are desirable; if not, whether we can break those conventions without producing even more stress. And those conventions are extensive, for they include not only the suppression of negative emotion but also the expression of other traditional values such as loyalty, patriotism and adherence to a national or social set of values.

3. Whenever you are faced with a difficult, stressful situation, the fact which should be uppermost in your mind is that *you* are living *your* life and *you* have the final power of decision over what you do with it. Some people find it difficult to accept that they have the ability to make autonomous choices and decisions without reference to other people. Each decision they make becomes the source of a great deal of stress because of the real or imagined consequences which it will have upon other people who should have no influence. This is not to suggest that one's family are of no importance or relevance in such decisions, because a sense of responsibility and duty towards people who depend emotionally or financially on you *is* important. Rather, it implies that one should have the power to avoid making decisions on the basis of irrelevant considerations.

4. Remember that your mind is designed to serve you, not to control you. Once you make a decision to banish stress from your life, that is what should happen. Furthermore, there is no need to become angry, depressed, worried or otherwise emotionally disturbed under stress. Such emotions only act as the source of further stress, and various effective techniques for dealing with them will be described throughout the book.

5. Don't tackle problems head on. Anyone who reacts to problems by violently fighting against them has probably overlooked the fact that reason and emotion do not work well when they are in conflict. Indeed, finding the solution to a problem only rarely involves a head-on attack, and a carefully worked out plan which allows you to side-step difficulties as they arise can be much more effective. Remember also that all of us occasionally meet problems which seem insuperable, and we can avoid a lot of frustration if we accept that there are certain things we cannot do (although this is not an excuse for avoiding responsibility).

HOW TO REDUCE YOUR LEVEL OF STRESS   45

6. Don't judge yourself by external standards. A man or woman whose self-esteem rests upon their ability to measure up to external standards is likely to be under a great deal of stress. For example, a person whose feeling of self-worth depends upon the favourable opinions of other people will be constantly on the look out for clues as to their attitude to him and fearful of the rejection which seems to indicate he is lacking as a person. A man or woman who is a perfectionist and believes that everything must be done perfectly will rarely be able to achieve the standards necessary for self-approval. But we do not have to spend our lives trying to measure up or prove ourselves adequate and competent: a satisfactory level of self-esteem and confidence provide all the feelings of value which a person needs. We shall return to this in Chapter 11.

7. In view of the different categories of mistaken belief mentioned earlier, you will no doubt realise that increasing one's self-confidence and overcoming dependency are of major importance in avoiding stress. Perhaps one reason why people are dependent on others is that they see in them something which they themselves lack, and hope to become more complete through the relationship. But such strategies rarely work for long, since no relationship can substitute for one's own feelings of self-worth.

8. Don't inflate the importance of past experience. Man is so subject to his emotions that events from many years ago may come to memory and cause anxiety and embarrassment, for example. But, in truth, *what has happened in the past does not matter*. No set of circumstances is ever exactly the same as a previous one, a fact which supports the idea that it is better to plan for the future on an intellectual basis rather than an emotional one.

9. 'Know Thyself.' In its ultimate meaning, this expression implies total understanding and acceptance of your thoughts, feelings and emotions; not, however, a passive acceptance of whatever happens in your mind, but an understanding so deep that you have the ability to use the activity of your mind as your servant, not your master.

10. Be flexible in life. It is no use engaging in useless conflict even if you are certain you are right. A change of plans or finding a more suitable environment can help avoid stress.

If you do experience stress, but find a process of examining your beliefs and attitudes proves unsuccessful, then you can lessen its effects by using deep relaxation (Chapter 3).

REFERENCES

Woolfolk, R. and Richardson, F. (1979). *Stress, Sanity and Survival*, p. 75. Futura, London.

3. Stress and Relaxation

Relaxation is a safe, simple and effective technique which increases the activity of the parasympathetic branch of the autonomic nervous system. You may recall from Chapter 1 that the parasympathetic system is also called the 'rest-digest' system because it lowers the body's level of arousal and therefore counteracts stress and tension.

Later in the chapter, we shall discuss in detail how you can use relaxation to reduce the effects of stress in your daily routine. First of all, however, we shall describe how you can learn to relax whenever you want.

There are several methods of relaxation. We have selected two of the easiest and most successful. Which of these is more suitable for you will depend partly on your personal preference and partly on how stressed you are. In fact we make some suggestions about this later on, so please read through the whole chapter before trying either method. If the method you have chosen does not seem to work very well, then try the other. But be sure to practise consistently – the best results seem to be obtained by relaxing for about 15 or 20 minutes twice a day. Obviously, the times you choose will depend on your daily routine, but it does help to keep them regular. If you have trouble sleeping, you may find that practising in bed at night not only helps to overcome your insomnia but also makes your sleep more refreshing and revitalising. (A word of caution here, though: remember that your aim is to develop the ability to relax at will, so dropping off to sleep before you have completed the relaxation procedure will defeat the object of the exercise. If you find that this is happening, you can sit in a chair or perhaps deliberately not make yourself too comfortable.)

Most people learn to relax on a bed, a sofa or an armchair. If you use a bed or sofa, you will probably find it best to lie on your back in a comfortable position with all parts of your body well supported. Your legs should be slightly apart with your feet angled outwards and your arms should be away from the sides of your body. It sometimes helps to place a cushion under the knees and to support the head in a similar way. If you use a chair, we suggest that you sit comfortably upright with your legs slightly apart and your feet flat on the floor. Your arms should rest on the arms of the chair with your palms downwards and your fingers slightly apart. You may experience slight discomfort if you try any deep relaxation procedure when you have a full stomach or when you are wearing tight clothing. It is therefore advisable to wait two hours after a meal, and to take off a tie and your shoes, for example, before you start.

Above all, remember that the most important thing is to be peaceful, calm and comfortable. If any of these suggestions cause you discomfort or are otherwise unsuitable, you can adapt them as you feel fit.

You are probably already aware that there is a close link between breathing out and relaxation. Exhalation is, in fact, essentially a process of muscular relaxation. You can make use of this relationship in the relaxation procedures below, by relaxing your muscles as you breathe out. But don't overdo it; breathing too quickly or too deeply for too long may cause dizziness.

With either Method A or Method B, start by closing your eyes and relaxing as much as you consciously can. At this stage, random thoughts may come flooding into your mind, but don't be disturbed by this – worrying will only increase your tension and arousal. Simply let the thoughts 'float away', and if your mind wanders, bring it gently back to the matter in hand without feeling upset or irritated.

METHOD A

This is the simpler of the two methods and works well for people who are already able to distinguish between muscular tension and relaxation.

STRESS AND RELAXATION

You start by transferring your attention over the different parts of your body in turn. As you become aware of each part, you discover whether the muscles are tense or relaxed. If there is tension present, you relax and 'let it go'. Obviously your muscles can safely relax more than they normally would because your body is fully supported, and you needn't spare a thought for essential processes like your heartbeat or breathing, because these are controlled automatically by the brain.

Relaxation like this is not a process of overt conscious effort; rather, it is a process of 'letting it happen'. It may help you to understand this point more clearly if you think of the act of tensing and relaxing your arm. Tensing the arm involves effort; relaxing the arm does not – it is a passive process, one that you are now extending to muscles of which you are normally not aware.

You will find it easier to keep your mind on what you are doing if you pass your attention over your body in a particular sequence. Don't spend too long on each muscle group, though; between 30 seconds and a minute is probably long enough. Remember that whenever you notice any tension you should relax and let it go. Each time you do this, let the feelings of relaxation spread and grow stronger.

Start with your fingers. Let them become relaxed, curved and limp. Then check for tension in your hands. Let them relax also. Feel this relaxation passing up your arms, and your arms resting more heavily on the bed or chair as they do so.

Move on to your neck and shoulders. These areas, like the face and back, attract a great deal of tension in most people. You may at this point be surprised to find how tense you really are. Relax your neck and shoulders so that the tension becomes less and less noticeable. Your head may feel heavier and seem to press into the bed or chair as your neck relaxes. Let all tension go as much as possible – and then let it go even further.

Next, think of your face. Your eyebrows and jaw muscles may be especially tense. Relax them. Let all tension go completely. Allow your tongue to relax loosely, your mouth to hang open slightly, and your face to assume a relaxed, blank expression.

Transfer your attention to your chest, abdomen and back. These are parts of your body where you may find it very helpful to use the association of breathing out and relaxation. Thus, each time you breathe out, you should feel yourself relaxing. And when you have finished each exhalation, you can let your body continue relaxing.

Relax your buttocks and thighs, and then your calves and ankles. Your feet and legs, like other parts of your body will feel heavier as the muscles relax more and more.

When you have relaxed each part of your body in turn, transfer your attention to your body as a whole. Let any remaining tension go. Then relax even more.

Once you have spent some time on this series of events, you may find that some tension has returned to various parts of your body. If so, simply relax your mind and body once again. Repeat this sequence several times if necessary. Although your first attempts at relaxation may leave you with the feeling that you have achieved nothing, keep going! You will probably be surprised at how little practice is required to become expert at the whole procedure.

METHOD B

If you have become habituated to a fairly constant level of stress and muscular tension, you may not be able to feel the difference between tension and relaxation, in which case you should adopt this slightly different procedure when learning how to relax. The preparatory steps and the order in which you relax the muscles of your body is similar to that used in Method A, but this procedure involves direct conscious effort before relaxation: you tense up each group of muscles before letting them 'flop' completely. In this way, you quickly come to distinguish between unpleasant feelings of tension and pleasant feelings of relaxation.

One question which often arises is: 'How much tension should one induce in each muscle group?' This depends on what you are comfortable with – there is little point in making your muscles so tense that they hurt! (In fact that may actually reduce the effectiveness of the procedure.) You must simply be able to distinguish between tension and relaxation.

Below, we describe one sequence of muscular tension and relaxation suitable for this method. The procedure is the same for each muscle group: tense the muscles, hold for about five seconds, then relax. It may be easier if you relax as you breathe out. Another useful idea is to mentally repeat the phrase 'This tension is all going away' as you tense and relax each muscle group. If you try this, you should think 'This tension is all . . .' as you tense your muscles and '. . . going away' as you relax them.

You need to spend some time – 30 seconds to a minute, say – simply paying attention to the feelings of relaxation which you induce in each muscle group. This will develop your ability to distinguish between tension and relaxation – and so help you to identify even slight muscular tension.

Here is the system of muscle tension and relaxation. Take your time and repeat each step as often as you think necessary.

Clench your fists. Squeeze. Pause . . . and relax.

Press your arms hard down on to the bed or chair. Pause . . . and relax.

Try to touch your shoulders with your wrists. Feel the tension. Pause . . . and relax.

Shrug your shoulders as high as possible. Pause . . . and relax.

Press your neck and head down into the bed or back into the chair. Build up the tension. Pause . . . relax.

Screw up your face: purse your lips; clench your jaw; press your tongue against the roof of your mouth; frown; screw your eyelids shut. Pause . . . and relax.

You may not feel very comfortable with all the muscles of your face under tension at the same time. If so, tense up the different areas of your face in sequence rather than simultaneously.

The muscles of the chest, abdomen and back are often particularly tense in individuals under stress, and it may therefore take slightly longer for you to learn how to relax them completely. When you push your stomach out, you tense up your abdomen; when you squeeze your buttocks together, you tense not only those muscles but also those in your back. Repeat this alternation of tension-relaxation several times in both areas, ensuring that you relax when you breathe out.

Finally, tense your legs and feet. You can do this by pressing the heels of your feet down into the bed or floor, and by stretching both legs straight out while flexing your toes back towards your shins.

As your ability to relax increases, you can gradually drop the tension part of the technique, and simply pass your attention over your body, letting the muscles relax as you do so. When you have learnt to relax all the separate areas of your body, you should then be able to achieve overall physical relaxation quickly and easily.

NOTES FOR BOTH METHODS

Relaxation is a skill, and it takes time to learn how to do it. One of the reasons for this is that distracting thoughts tend to enter your mind while you practise, although these fall away as your ability continues to develop. Remember that relaxing is not like other physical activities. It is a 'happening' rather than a 'doing'. Conscious thoughts such as: 'Am I doing this right?' or 'I should be preparing dinner!' are going to increase your arousal and counteract relaxation. You need to resolve that you won't worry about the time you spend relaxing, that you can take the phone off the hook and not answer the door, and that you have a right to ask your family to leave you alone while you practise.

Some of the effects of physical relaxation may be unfamiliar to you. For example, your muscles may feel warm or cold, may tingle or vibrate, or may give small jerks or twitches. These are signs that you are succeeding! (If you feel too cold you should obviously use a blanket or heat the room.) More importantly, however, when your whole body is relaxed, you tend to feel either as if you are floating or as if you are sinking down and down, deeper and deeper, into the bed or chair. These unusual but enjoyable sensations need not disturb you. They develop because the brain cannot correctly interpret signals from pressure-sensitive nerve endings in the skin while the body is more or less motionless.

When physically relaxed, some people like to remain calm

with random thoughts drifting through their minds, while others find that visualising some particular mental image such as a beach or a countryside scene helps them to remain relaxed. If you do this, try to feel as though you are actually a part of the scene, and not just a detached observer. Yet another possibility is simply to repeat the word 'relax' each time you breathe out, a technique which is often helpful in the early stages of the procedure.

After you have completed a session of relaxation, don't suddenly resume your normal activity. Stretch each part of your body to accustom the muscles to physical action once again and get up slowly.

GENERAL COMMENTS

There are many people who know they need to take action to preserve their mental or physical health but who claim that they are 'too busy' to relax. In fact this remark is usually an excuse from someone who can't be bothered to learn the technique, because even a very busy person can practise relaxation in bed before going to sleep.

So why might someone not bother to help him- or herself? There are many possible reasons. To start with, the technique involves doing something for oneself. Some individuals are too lazy to take such positive steps. Others might think that 'it won't work for me'. Whether or not that is true depends chiefly on your motivation. It is not just our opinion that relaxation can relieve stress: there is plenty of evidence to back up the fact. Therefore, if you are determined to avoid the harmful effects of stress by learning to relax, avoid them you will!

WHEN AND HOW TO USE THE RELAXATION TECHNIQUE

As we have suggested, relaxing before your night's sleep reduces your level of arousal and so helps you to obtain refreshing and revitalising sleep. The full relaxation technique can also be helpful if you wake during the night or in the morning with feelings of anxiety and tension. During the night, it is important not to worry about the fact that you are awake – doing so makes you less likely to sleep. Simply go through the whole process until you reach a state of mental calm and physical relaxation, during which you should at some point fall asleep once more.

If you want to relax in the morning, first of all get out of bed and do something which requires mental and physical activity, like making a cup of tea. This helps to stop you falling asleep again.

Even if you didn't use the technique for anything else, you would derive great benefit from a regular schedule of deep relaxation. This is because one or two sessions of relaxation each day reduce one's level of arousal, thereby making one much more calm and reversing all the effects of stress which we have already described. However, the most important aspect of the technique is unquestionably the way in which it provides a means of rapid relaxation for use at any time during the day.

RAPID RELAXATION FOR RELIEF FROM STRESS

When you discover – as you will at some point – that you have learnt to relax deeply and quickly, you can begin to use a form of *rapid relaxation* as a matter of routine during your everyday life. This application of relaxation (described below) is suitable for odd moments during the day and in fact need take no more than a minute or two, but it is still very effective in lowering one's level of arousal. Moreover, you can use it among other people, and no-one will know what you are doing (a fact which is sometimes important). We need hardly point out the potential benefits of keeping your arousal to a reasonable level. It is surely preferable to use a quick relaxation technique several times a day rather than develop the physical and psychological problems listed on page 17.

Of course, you may also wish to use the technique before and during situations which you find especially stressful so as to ensure that you remain much more calm and relaxed. Examples of such situations might be: before and during a meeting, examination or interview; while waiting for an appointment; before standing to deliver a speech; while speaking to people; and so on.

There are also benefits to be gained from using the technique *after* any stressful event such as a meeting, a car journey, a shopping trip, an interview, and so on. It can be especially useful to do this after your day's work but before driving home. That way, you won't tend to use your car as an outlet for your aggression, irritation and annoyance.

So how does the technique work? First of all, you will need to sit in a chair with your back straight, your arms positioned on the arms of the chair (or, if it doesn't have arms, hanging by the side of your body or resting on your lap), your feet flat on the floor and your head comfortably balanced. The aim is to relax as much as possible while sitting in this position. At least to start with, it may be necessary for you to tense all the muscles of your body before you relax. (Since this is a rapid relaxation technique, it is better to tense all the muscles of your body at once rather than in sequence.) But if you have mastered the skill of deep relaxation, you will soon find that you can relax just by thinking about it. One way of helping yourself to do this is to repeat silently the word 'relax' each time you breathe out. This should allow you to relax at will. And even if you are standing up, you should be able to relax much of your body.

The technique is extremely effective. Even if you do not relax completely, you will still lower your level of sympathetic arousal and therefore feel more calm and be able to think more clearly. However, we cannot emphasise sufficiently that to derive the maximum benefit from it, you must maintain your ability to relax at a high level of efficiency, and this will only happen if you remember to use the technique as many times as possible each day. Here are some examples of the times when you might wish to use rapid relaxation: while travelling in a train, bus or car; while waiting to be served in a shop; while speaking to people on the phone; and so on.

You may also find it extremely helpful to spend slightly longer relaxing at lunch-time, especially if your daily routine is highly stressed. For example, businessmen can lock their office doors and refresh themselves by relaxing for 10 or 15 minutes with their eyes closed. If you happen to lack privacy, it may be possible to do this in your car outside the office, or even in the loo!

By all means continue with sessions of deep relaxation if you wish; but the important thing about rapid relaxation is that it is suited to your daily routine – where stresses arise – and can be used among other people in your daytime environment with no disruption.

When you have been using relaxation techniques for some time, you should notice certain distinct changes in your life. First of all, you will probably experience periods of calmness, relaxation and associated effects such as improved interactions with other people and greater self-confidence. Your reaction to annoying, upsetting or distressing events and situations will also be less marked. These periods of relaxation and lessened stress should gradually spread throughout your day. Perhaps, at first, the moments of greatest stress in your life may not appear much different, but soon you should notice a decrease in your arousal even at the worst moments of stress.

Don't expect sudden and dramatic changes. You could hardly hope for that, especially if you have become habituated to constant stress and tension. Rather, remember that a decrease in the frequency, duration or intensity of stress-related problems is an improvement. Thus, if your tension headaches occur once a day instead of three times, that is an improvement. So too, if they do not last as long or if they are not as severe.

RELAXATION OR SELF-HYPNOSIS?

It has been said that methods of relaxation such as that described above are better used as a preventive treatment rather than a cure. In a sense, there is some truth in that remark. For example, where some more fundamental personality or anxiety problem underlies the emotional and physical symptoms of stress, we may be justified in regarding *relaxation* as a way of relieving symptoms and *self-hypnosis* as a way of tackling the underlying problem. This is why we have discussed methods of self-hypnosis in Chapter 4. Later in the book, we explain how self-hypnosis can be used to help overcome anxiety, depression and personality problems such as a lack of confidence. One of the most obvious points in favour of self-hypnosis is its flexibility: it can be used for a combination of problems, yet there is no reason why it cannot be used for relief from stress, alongside – or instead of – straightforward relaxation techniques.

4. Hypnosis, Self-Hypnosis and the Tape Recorder Technique

Deep relaxation is an effective treatment for some forms of stress, but needs to be complemented by other techniques for tackling emotional and personality problems such as depression, anxiety, lack of confidence and feelings of inferiority. One such technique is self-hypnosis. This provides the easiest and most effective way of getting into contact with your subconscious, the part of your mind which controls the way you think and feel. However, before using the technique for your own benefit, you will need to know what hypnosis is and how it works.

Normally, when somebody makes a suggestion, we consciously think whether or not we will accept it. The same applies, of course, to suggestions which we make to ourselves. Thus, for example, simply telling yourself that you do not feel depressed will not remove the symptoms of depression because your conscious mind considers and tests the suggestion. It realises 'this isn't true' and the suggestion is rejected. In hypnosis, however, this 'critical factor' of the conscious mind is switched off so that suggestions can pass straight into the subconscious. How is this suspension of the critical factor achieved?

When a hypnotherapist treats a client, he may ask the client to concentrate on breathing slowly and deeply, or on keeping his eyes fixed on one spot in front of him. While the conscious attention of the client is fully occupied in this way, any suggestions which the hypnotherapist makes cannot be tested, but will pass straight into the subconscious. The hypnotherapist suggests that his client is relaxing more and more, finding it more and more difficult to keep his eyes open, that he is feeling more and more relaxed. These and other suggestions, of a more therapeutic kind, can pass into the subconscious which accepts them to a degree depending on how active or inactive the critical factor of the conscious mind might have been. It is obvious that the client must be willing to co-operate. If he is reluctant to accept these suggestions, or tries to analyse his feelings and experience, he will not pass into hypnosis.

Although there are other methods of hypnosis, they are all based on this principle. You might well ask what exactly is happening during the 'switching-off' of the critical factor. The surprising answer is that no-one really knows. However, the characteristics of hypnosis *are* known. Firstly, as already mentioned, a person must be willing to co-operate. Secondly, hypnosis is not sleep. Although conscious awareness is reduced, at another level the mind still knows exactly what is going on and no-one can be made to do anything against his or her will. (This applies also to the appalling acts of stage hypnotists in which people are 'made to' carry out ludicrous acts for the audience's entertainment. There is ample evidence that people do those acts because they are willing to co-operate. If they are told to do something which they find unacceptable, they return automatically to normal awareness.) Thirdly, suggestions made during hypnosis are acted upon when a person has returned to normal consciousness – this is why it can help overcome emotional and personal problems. Fourthly, everyone can enter hypnosis, although a small number of people have difficulty at first, probably because they have a subconscious fear of not being in control of themselves. However, someone in hypnosis is not in any danger of 'losing control' and talking about his innermost secrets and desires. He will do this only if he wants to do so. Equally, whether or not you consciously forget what you have said or heard during hypnosis depends entirely upon whether or not the therapist (or you) wants this to happen.

Having an idea of what hypnosis consists of, let us now turn to its use in self-hypnosis. The principle is exactly the same as in hypnosis, except that you are your own therapist! Before discussing the methods by which self-hypnosis can be used to influence the subconscious mind and alter behaviour patterns, we need to consider how often self-hypnosis actually works. It does have its limitations; this is a fair and reasonable statement. Firstly, there are those people who have the fear of losing control described above. They may need professional help to learn how to induce self-hypnosis, although we shall offer some possible solutions to the problem later on. Secondly, some people will always deceive themselves that they wish to improve psychologically, while in actual fact they have no real desire to do so. (For example, a woman may not really wish to recover from a depression because she can manipulate people with her illness (see p. 93).) Clearly, such people will not make a genuine effort to learn self-hypnosis. Thirdly, there are a few cases of psychological difficulties which stem from repressed trauma. We have already briefly covered the idea of repression, and the question now, therefore, is whether self-hypnosis designed to change a person's behaviour can work without taking account of any past trauma. There is very good evidence, in fact, that very nearly all emotional problems are helped by self-hypnosis, and that even when repressed trauma are affecting adult life, self-hypnosis can assist an individual to come to terms with them. For reasons which will later become obvious, we must postpone further discussion of this question.

All hypnosis is made up of four steps:

1. Induction of the hypnotic state
2. Therapeutic suggestions to influence the subconscious
3. Suggestions to come back to normal awareness or consciousness
4. Application of the hypnotic suggestions in everyday life

You may have realised already the biggest problem of self-hypnosis. As soon as you make any therapeutic suggestions to yourself, you must use your conscious mind. This alerts your 'critical factor' which either brings you back to normal consciousness or rejects the suggestions. The easiest way to overcome this problem is to use a tape recorder; it is also the most effective method of self-hypnosis. We shall describe this first, then consider other possibilities and finally discuss them all in general terms.

I: THE TAPE RECORDER TECHNIQUE

This effective method is also very simple: you obtain a cassette recorder, record the induction, hypnotic and 'coming out' suggestions, and then sit or lie down and play the tape.

60 HYPNOSIS, AND THE TAPE RECORDER TECHNIQUE

Assuming that you have learnt the induction technique correctly, you will undoubtedly be able to go deep enough into hypnosis for the suggestions to be highly effective. The induction technique which suits most people is progressive relaxation. Obviously, if you have already learnt deep relaxation for stress relief, you will be able to go into hypnosis on your first attempt. If you have not, it will perhaps take a little longer to learn self-hypnosis. However, by far the most important factor in the effectiveness of self-help therapy is your determination to make it work. Here is the procedure.

1. Obtain a cassette recorder. This is more convenient than a reel-to-reel machine and a 90–minute cassette will leave plenty of room for all your recording. Most people find that it is worth spending slightly more to obtain a good-quality machine. At first sight, the investment seems high, but when you consider what you hope to achieve and the cost of professional help, you will realise it is not. If you make excuses about time, money or opportunity, you should perhaps give careful consideration to the possibility that you do not wish to change.

The content of the induction section of the tape is directly related to the method of listening to the self-hypnosis tape. We must therefore digress slightly to cover the procedure used for listening to a self-hypnosis tape.

2. You will be listening to the tape lying flat on a bed, fully supported in the manner described for deep relaxation. Alternatively, you may sit in an easy chair with your back straight and well supported, in which case you will have your head balanced nicely and your arms on the arms of the chair with your fingers slightly apart. Your legs should also be slightly apart, feet flat on the floor in front of you. It is, however, preferable to lie full length.

In either case, the room should be neither too hot nor too cold, too dim nor too bright, and certainly not noisy. You might wish to take the phone off the hook and resolve not to answer the door if the bell rings. In any event pick a time when you are unlikely to be disturbed. A useful and helpful procedure is to obtain a pair of cushioned headphones which plug into the cassette recorder. This will keep your recorded message private and shut out external noises.

HYPNOSIS, AND THE TAPE RECORDER TECHNIQUE

3. Leave a minute or two blank at the start of the tape and then record your induction material as shown below. The entire induction procedure should initially take about 15 minutes but can gradually be shortened as you become more expert. (You may thus need to re-record your tape from time to time.) At any stage, the important thing is that you are happy with what you have recorded. You should speak slowly and clearly into the microphone in a relaxing, gentle, pleasant monotone. There are two alternative induction scripts given below. One or other will suit you better; you will probably be able to add your own suggestions. In both Script A and Script B, you may find it helpful to repeat each of sections 4–7 several times, and to pause between each phrase in sections 10 and 11 so that you have time to feel each effect that is mentioned. Both these scripts are written as though a therapist were taking you through hypnosis.

SQUARE BRACKETS ARE USED TO INDICATE INSTRUCTIONS WHICH SHOULD NOT BE RECORDED IN THE TAPE, for example [pause].

INDUCTION SCRIPT 'A'

1. Settle down comfortably and make sure that your head, neck, shoulders, arms and legs are all settled comfortably.

2. Close your eyes. Start breathing slowly and deeply, and each time that you breathe out, allow yourself to relax more and more.

3. You will now hear only my voice and feel only what I tell you to feel until after you wake up.

4. Concentrate on your breathing. Keep up that slow, steady, regular pattern of deep breathing.

5. And as you breathe out, allow yourself to relax more and more. Don't concentrate on my words, simply allow yourself to relax. Relaxing peacefully, pleasantly, and comfortably, each time you breathe out.

6. Each time you breathe out, let yourself relax deeper and deeper. As I continue speaking to you, you will find that you are able to sink down deeper, deeper and deeper. *Relax*

62 HYPNOSIS, AND THE TAPE RECORDER TECHNIQUE

your mind, *relax* your body, relax your whole nervous system *completely*. *Feel* yourself relaxing more and more peacefully, pleasantly and comfortably.

7. As I continue speaking to you now, your eyelids will become very heavy and tired. And as they become heavier and heavier, and more and more tired, so your mind will become drowsier and more relaxed, letting yourself go utterly and completely, relaxing deeper and deeper, becoming loose and limp everywhere. As your eyelids continue to lock themselves tighter and tighter to your cheeks, your mind continues to become drowsier and drowsier and more relaxed all the time. [You may substitute the word 'sleepier' for 'more relaxed' if you prefer, so long as you understand that 'sleep' is only a convenient expression rather than a specific instruction.]

8. As you feel your eyelids getting heavier and heavier, they are relaxing more and more, and you know that they are so relaxed they will not open. When I ask you to, I want you to test them to make certain of this. Want it to happen, expect it to happen and let it happen. Now test them gently to make certain they won't open.

9. Now, *relax, relax, relax*.

10. Concentrate on your right [left (use the dominant hand)] hand. In a few seconds, one of the fingers is going to begin jerking a little all by itself or is going to tingle or pulse. Don't be surprised when this happens, simply accept it and allow it to happen. Don't try to make it happen, simply relax and let it happen.

    One of the fingers is now beginning to jerk or tingle. And as it does so, you are allowing your hand to become lighter and lighter, and as it becomes lighter and lighter you are allowing it to rise into the air. As it rises into the air, you accept what is happening and you find your body feels heavier and heavier. Your hand and arm are lighter and lighter, your legs and body heavier and heavier. All the time your hand and arm are rising higher and higher, as though your arm was tied to a balloon. In a few seconds' time, I am going to count from five to one, and when I reach

HYPNOSIS, AND THE TAPE RECORDER TECHNIQUE

one, your arm will suddenly flop and fall on to the bed [chair] beside you. As it does so, all tension in your body will go away completely and you will be completely relaxed and calm. And now I am going to count five-four-three-two-one – completely relaxed, all tension gone away completely.

INDUCTION SCRIPT 'B'

Stages 1–9 are the same as Script 'A'.

10. Now your whole body is relaxing even more deeply than before. To help it relax, imagine that a powerful anaesthetic has been injected into your arm and that it is spreading all round your body.
    [pause]
    Feel it happen. Imagine that powerful anaesthetic passing all round your body. It is now moving through both your arms making them feel numb and heavy. As the feelings of numbness and heaviness spread, you will know that you are relaxing deeper and deeper. The anaesthetic is now moving up into your neck, face and head. Imagine it spreading out and relaxing all the muscles of your neck, face and head. As they relax, they feel numb and heavy.
    [pause]
    Imagine the anaesthetic moving into your chest and stomach, making all the muscles relax completely. Feel these muscles become relaxed and heavy as it spreads throughout your whole body.
    [pause]
    It is now flowing down through your back and legs, making them relaxed and heavy and taking away all tension of every kind.
    Relax, Relax, Relax.

SCRIPTS 'A' AND 'B' ONWARDS

11. Now the feeling of relaxation is spreading to your mind and body and you find it so much more pleasant and calm that you allow yourself to sink deeper and deeper. In a moment I am going to ask you to take five deep breaths which will relax you and send you even deeper. As you take each deep

breath and exhale, let the feeling of relaxation pass through your whole body and release all tension. When you take the fifth deep breath and exhale, you will relax even more, and all tension in mind or body will go away completely. [While recording the following, spread out the words so that 'this tension is all' can extend over inhalation, and 'going away' over exhalation.]

Now, breathe in deeply and then exhale. As you do so, this tension is all [pause] going away [pause]. Now, breathe in deeply and then exhale. As you do so, this tension is all [pause] going away [pause]. Now, breathe in deeply and then exhale. As you do so, this tension is all [pause] going away [pause]. Now, breathe in deeply and then exhale. As you do so, this tension is all [pause] going away [pause]. Now, breathe in deeply and then exhale. As you do so, this tension has all [pause] gone away completely.

12. Now my words will act as a powerful signal which will allow you to feel safe, relaxed, comfortable and happy. All the time I am speaking to you, my words will act as a powerful signal making you relax more and more. You can allow your mind to wander on to any subject which it wants to, but if it does not wander that is not important. Simply continue relaxing mentally and physically until I tell you otherwise. If you need to awaken quickly in an emergency, you will always do so.

That is the induction process. Details of the specific treatments which may now be applied can be found in each relevant chapter. Here is a general treatment for relaxation, stress relief, increased feelings of confidence and well-being. It is recorded in the same, relaxing, gentle voice as the induction process.

STAGE 2 – TREATMENT

You are relaxing deeper and deeper all the time that I am speaking to you. You know that you are relaxing very well and so you will feel much better and refreshed when this session ends. As you relax more and more each time you use this technique, you will carry more and more of this relaxation through into your everyday life. This means that after each session of self-hypnosis you feel more calm and relaxed and mentally relaxed. Your mind is clearer. People do not upset you as much. As you feel more relaxed, more able to cope, you also feel less and less tense and irritable. Relaxation will help you to do all of this, and as the feelings of relaxation which you learn with this technique spread through your daily life more and more, you will also feel more and more self-confident. But the most important way in which deep relaxation can help you is by allowing your mind and body to remain less tense in your daily life. You will find yourself using only the muscles you need for whatever you are doing, while the remainder of your body is relaxed. Because you have learnt a habit of tension, these improvements will only develop gradually at first, but more and more powerfully with each day that goes by. If you feel yourself becoming tense in your body or mind, you can relax by using the five deep breaths [see p. 67], which always act as a very powerful signal to take away all tension of any kind. As the days go by, you become more relaxed and confident. This prevents tension from building up in your mind or body. You feel less and less tense all the time now. Soon all tension will have gone away completely. And another benefit is that you feel more confident and able to cope with life. If your habit of becoming tense shows itself, you can relax and cope quite easily. Soon you will find yourself doing things which previously you thought you could not do, feeling calm, relaxed and confident, knowing that the five deep breaths will take away all tension of any kind. You will also find that your sleep at night becomes more and more refreshing and relaxing. You will begin to sleep better and better each time you go to bed. You will worry less and less about problems. You will worry less and less about not sleeping. You will wake up feeling more and more refreshed each morning. Relax now until I tell you to wake up.

STAGE 3 – WAKING UP (continue the recording as below)

And each time that you go into self-hypnosis, or relax, you will relax deeper and deeper. Each time you find yourself going deeper than ever before. You can do this because you look forward to your sessions of relaxation, knowing that they are working well for you. And in a moment, I am going to bring you back to full awareness. You will want to wake up and be able to wake up as I count from one to ten. Starting now. One, Two. You are gradually coming back into a lighter sleep. Three, Four. Your body is beginning to regain feeling. Five, Six. You are waking up more and more all the time now, coming back into a lighter, lighter sleep. Seven, Eight. You are coming back into a lighter sleep, feeling fine, refreshed and happy. Nine, Ten. Getting ready to wake up now. Coming back into a lighter sleep, getting ready to wake up when I say 'now', getting ready to open your eyes, feeling refreshed and fine in every way – NOW ... NOW ... NOW. Open your eyes now, feeling relaxed and refreshed.

HINTS ON INDUCTION

Most people find that either of the two methods described above is perfectly satisfactory. A few, however, have personalities which are not attuned to either method. Some people do not like an authoritarian tone of voice and need a 'permissive' induction technique which 'asks for' the co-operation of the subject. An example of this would be 'and now I want you to become more relaxed' instead of 'and now you are becoming more relaxed'. There is only one way you can find out – and that is to try it for yourself. Other people, as we mentioned earlier, have 'rigid' personalities and cannot easily go into hypnosis. A useful tip for such people, which may also help others who find it difficult to relax without the security of a therapist, is to give the conscious mind another task besides concentrating on deep breathing, so that the suggestions on the tape are more readily accepted. You can do this by counting down from five hundred to one while playing a tape of Script 'B'. You shouldn't make any effort, or try to listen to the tape, but just count down. If you lose your place, just start again at the first number that comes into your mind. You will find that as you count, your most tense muscles start to relax – your stomach, or neck, perhaps. Remember that feelings of relaxation are always preferable to feelings of tension and strain.

One of these methods will work if your motivation is high. However, if you still have difficulty, you may be able to adapt one of the autosuggestion methods for use with the tape recorder technique, and the general notes at the end of this chapter may also be helpful.

HINTS ON THE FIVE DEEP BREATHS

You can use the five deep breaths during the day as a signal to relieve mental and physical tension. This is because your mind will associate five deep breaths and the words 'This tension is all going away' with mental and physical relaxation. To use the technique:

STOP what you are doing.
Consciously relax as much as possible in mind or body.
Breathe in slowly and deeply while thinking (or, if you prefer, saying):
  'This tension is all . . .
and exhale, allowing yourself to relax as you do so, while thinking:
  going away.'
REPEAT this four times, and on the fifth change the words to:
  'This tension has all gone away completely.'

The effectiveness of this procedure depends very much on your concentrating on using it effectively, and not repeating the words quickly and superficially. The more you use the five deep breaths, the more benefit they will be to you. Remember, therefore, to use them as often as possible.

HINTS ON THE THERAPEUTIC SUGGESTIONS

You will find specific ideas for these suggestions in later chapters, but you can easily make up your own by following a few simple rules.

Make your suggestions gradual, and try to find the correct suggestion pattern. For example, a man who wished to stop smoking might find hypnosis had no effect if he recorded: 'You are now stopping smoking completely. You will never want another cigarette.' This is clearly foolish because he will be physically dependent on cigarettes, and unable to give them up suddenly. He may also be psychologically dependent on them, and so, even if the suggestion did work, giving up cigarettes would produce anxiety. However, if he recorded, 'All the time now, you are finding that you need cigarettes less and less often, less and less severely', he would probably have had some success.

The suggestion should be positive, rather than negative. A person lacking in self-confidence would not want to record 'I shall not worry about the opinions of others.' Instead, he might record 'I feel more and more confident whenever I am with people, even if I sense they do not like me.' This last example also demonstrates another point. A few people find it difficult to relate to a tape which they have recorded in the second person, 'you'. If you find that this is a problem, why not try regarding the voice on the tape as a therapist speaking to you, or as you being a therapist and addressing your own subconscious? If this fails to impress you, try recording the tape in the first person substituting 'I' for you. And if this fails – but it is highly unlikely to do so – try one of the other methods of self-hypnosis: autosuggestion or visualisation.

II: AUTOSUGGESTION

Some people may find it impossible to obtain or use a tape recorder. Nevertheless, self-hypnosis can still be useful, particularly autosuggestion. This is a process of self-hypnosis in which you make therapeutic suggestions to yourself before you sink down into a deeply relaxed state which corresponds to Stage 2 in the tape recorder technique. It is possible to use either of the induction methods described earlier by changing the instructions into the first person, for example, 'I am sinking down deeper and deeper.' The problem is that the conscious mind checks that this is actually happening. Here is a compromise that overcomes this difficulty, and which can also be used with the tape recorder technique if so desired.

Fix your gaze upon one spot on the ceiling (if you are lying down) or on the opposite wall (if you are sitting in a chair). This spot should be slightly above eye level towards the top of your head, a position which naturally produces tension in the eye muscles, and makes them feel heavy, so that they eventually begin to close. Mentally make the following induction statements several times each:

1. *My eyelids are becoming heavier.*
2. *They are heavy and tired and I cannot keep them open.*
3. *I am allowing my eyes to close.*
   Now breathe slowly and deeply. Repeat mentally:
4. *Each time I breathe out, I am becoming more relaxed.*
   Allow yourself to feel relaxed. Pass your attention over each muscle group in turn. As your attention moves over each muscle group, simply think:
5. *My (hands) are becoming relaxed and heavy.*
   Do this in turn for your hands, arms, shoulders, neck, face, head, chest, stomach, back, legs and feet. After you have made each suggestion, immediately move on to the next area of your body.
   You should then repeat:
6. *Each time I breathe out, the feeling of heaviness increases.*
   Do not check to see whether it is happening or you will alert your critical factor. Simply accept that it will happen, that it is happening and that you want it to happen.

Then, when you are comfortably relaxed, practise the use of the five deep breaths. As we described in the tape recorder technique, this involves breathing in and out slowly five times. On the first four cycles of inhalation and exhalation, mentally repeat the words 'This tension is all . . .' as you breathe in, and '. . . going away' as you breathe out. On the fifth, mentally repeat 'This tension has all . . .' as you breathe in, and '. . . gone away completely' as you breathe out. While you do this, allow feelings of relaxation to overcome you and spread throughout your body.

Once you feel confident of your ability to relax deeply and quickly, you will be in a position to make use of autosuggestion proper. To do this, formulate your therapeutic suggestion in advance, and mentally repeat it several times just before the five deep breaths. The five deep breaths then act as a quick trigger to induce self-hypnosis, after which you should allow your mind to wander on to any subject it wishes. The method works because the conscious mind has no chance to examine the suggestion critically before the five deep breaths take you into hypnosis. The subconscious can act upon the suggestion even though you may not be aware of it, and if you follow the technique correctly it will work well. Another useful tip to deepen the hypnotic state just after the five deep breaths is to imagine that you are riding down an unending escalator or repeating the word 'deeper'. Your self-hypnosis will become deeper, so that you may lose conscious awareness and your mind begins to wander. Alternatively, you may feel you have gone deep enough at some particular point. If so, stop there. You are always in control.

To emerge from self-hypnosis, all you have to do is simply think 'I now wish to return to full awareness. I shall count from one to ten, and, as I do so, gradually come back to normal awareness.' Then count up and make beneficial suggestions similar to those included in the tape recorder technique Stage 3.

III: VISUALISATION

This is really a development of autosuggestion. Almost without exception, people find that visualisation is the most powerful tool for changing their self-image, and it also forms the basis of self-help treatment for certain anxiety problems, particularly phobias. Perhaps its most important use is in self-help treatment for feelings of inferiority and lack of confidence. The method is simple enough: relax, use the five deep breaths, and then picture yourself in your imagination doing whatever you wish to achieve. The technique involves seeing and feeling yourself doing what you want to do, being what you want to be, and so on; not just thinking about it, but actually seeing and feeling it as though you were really doing it, not as though you were observing yourself doing it. This might include:

- being relaxed at a party
- confidently asserting yourself in a particular situation
- speaking confidently to strangers
- remaining calm in an exam
- winning a game of tennis
- picturing yourself as you would like to be after losing weight

IV: GENERAL DISCUSSION

REPRESSION

The most important question is whether self-hypnosis can overcome problems which result from past incidents that have been repressed. Psychoanalysts believe that it is necessary to identify and relive these events before adult problems can be cured. Is this true? The answer is a categoric 'No'. Recent psychological research shows that adult emotional and personal problems can be treated without examining past trauma. It is a matter of learning to relax, apply self-hypnosis (and other techniques as needed) for specific problems.

However, one cannot deny that there are a few cases where trauma is severe and makes self-hypnosis ineffective. One young man described by Peter Blythe (1976) had a severe perspiration problem. At home he could relax beautifully, but as soon as he went out, the perspiration became so bad that it left white stains on his shoes and clothes. The problem only stopped when he was regressed under hypnosis to relive the events which had caused the trauma. In this case, self-hypnosis with a suggestion that perspiration would gradually become less and less troublesome (say) would have been totally ineffective. However, one way of using self-hypnosis effectively would have been a regression to relive the past events and experiences. Unfortunately, this kind of 'abreaction' can be disturbing if not dangerous. A much better idea is to use self-hypnosis to gain greater understanding and insight into your emotional problems at a rate which you can handle. In other words, to record a tape along the lines of:

> You are gradually gaining insight and understanding into your emotional and personality problems. Each day now, your subconscious mind releases a little more of the memories which you have repressed. This will happen only as fast as your conscious mind is able to cope and understand them. As you recall the events and feelings which have caused your problems, you gain greater insight and understanding into the way you feel, think and behave. And as you do so, you will be more and more relaxed, calm and confident. You gradually understand your problems and they trouble you less and less

often, less and less severely all the time now. Very soon they will have gone away completely.

YOUR ATTITUDE OF MIND

All hypnosis is self-hypnosis in the sense that your willingness to co-operate is essential. Before you start, you must be prepared to record a tape and spend time experimenting until you find a formula which suits you. Then you must be prepared to go into self-hypnosis at least once a day – but the more often the better. One useful technique is to have two sessions of treatment, one immediately following the other. If you do this, you will get much more effect the second time around.

You need to extend your co-operation to a willingness to enter self-hypnosis. The summary of your attitude is 'want it to happen, expect it to happen and let it happen', but don't try to make it happen, push yourself or analyse the experience as it happens.

Don't worry if you feel you haven't gone very deep. It is notoriously difficult to judge the depth of a hypnotic state, and people often think they haven't 'gone deep' or 'been hypnotised at all'. Invariably they are wrong. A good way to check your hypnosis is to see how much of the counting-out procedure you remember. A light trance will enable you to recall the whole counting-out procedure, a deep one, very little of it. But although a deeper hypnosis may have a more rapid therapeutic effect (since your critical factor is less active), even a light trance will produce good results.

Don't set yourself up for failure in any of the following ways:

- By expecting instant results. Improvement takes time, but you should make steady, forward progress. Remember that improvement can be measured by reduction in intensity, duration or frequency of emotional problems.
- By giving up. You may not notice immediate improvement. Don't give up! Some people suddenly have a breakthrough some time after they start. You must also be aware that there may be setbacks, when your forward progress stops or reverses slightly. This depends on many factors, such as the amount of stress you experience. Simply accept what has

happened; above all, don't condemn or criticise yourself – simply carry on using the techniques.
- By rushing into situations you are not ready for. But that, of course, is not an excuse for avoiding them. Just take things one step at a time.
- By making excuses: 'I don't like the sound of my own voice on tape.' If this is so, get someone else to record the tape for you to a script which you have written.

  'It's too much trouble.' If you bought this book, what did you expect? A magic solution? There are none of those in life.

  'I don't like the idea of self-hypnosis.' This is a weak excuse if there ever was one. Self-hypnosis is safe, relaxing and beneficial.

  'It's dangerous.' If there is any emergency, you will return to full consciousness immediately. But if it troubles you, record on the induction tape: 'You will always wake up if there is a need to deal with an emergency.' Also, if you wish: 'You will remain relaxed and calm if the phone or doorbell rings.'
- By changing your self-hypnosis therapy too many times. Select one target at a time, and make it realistic and specific. Set a date by which you will achieve it.

Finally, be adventurous. Experiment with as many techniques as you need until you are able to relax completely. The section on deep relaxation has other useful ideas. Always remember: you are in control, not only of the use to which you put this technique, but also the benefits which you gain from it.

REFERENCE

Blythe, P. (1976). *Self-Hypnotism*, pp. 21–2. Arthur Barker, London.

5. Understanding Your Feelings and Emotions

We all know the word 'neurotic'. It occurs in conversation and everyday life again and again, usually as a slightly insulting description of a man or women with an emotional problem. In this sense, neurosis is neither clear cut nor well defined. However, there is another use of the word: the medical use, which tries to explain what neurosis is, where it comes from, and what it does to people. You can see that this use of the word implies that a neurosis can induce unusual patterns of behaviour – neurotic behaviour – in someone who is experiencing it. Bearing this point in mind, a neurosis can be defined as 'a state in which a person shows irrational, absurd, pointless or unproductive physical or emotional behaviour which he is unable to change by conscious effort, and which is associated with strong emotions'. Some definitions suggest a person recognises his own neurotic behaviour as irrational – although this may be true (as in phobias), equally it may not (as in some depressions).

There are three main types of neurosis: reactive depression, anxiety and phobias. This book sets out to show that anxiety and other emotional problems are an easily explained and normal part of living which can be alleviated by the person who experiences them. Understanding is half the battle in treating emotional problems, because a fear of the unknown is often an additional factor which makes anxiety or depression worse. Many simple self-help treatments are very effective, and medical help is needed only in the most severe cases. As for the origin of neurosis, we can be equally definite. Only a very few cases of emotional disorder are inherited genetically. It is true that the children of a neurotic adult are more likely to experience emotional problems, but this is only because a child

UNDERSTANDING YOUR FEELINGS AND EMOTIONS 75

learns how to behave by watching its parents and seeing how they respond to life events. When emotional problems are inherited, they are much more serious: they are called 'psychoses', and the most common forms are schizophrenia and manic-depressive illness. For the sake of illustration, manic-depressive illness is described in the chapter on depression; however, they are not common, nor are they amenable to self-help treatments, and so they fall outside the scope of this book.

Neuroses fall on to a spectrum of severity. The least severe are represented by the mild superstitions which we all share – even if we deny it – such as not walking under ladders or on the cracks in the pavements, a dislike of cats, and so on. A slightly worse neurosis is excessive worry. There are many people who worry more than is good for them. At school, they worry about exams, tests and teachers; at home, they worry about their friends and family; later in life, their career or finances become more important. The minor inconvenience of worried thoughts such as these contrasts sharply with an anxiety neurosis at its worst, when a person is irrationally worried to such an extent that he cannot function normally.

Perhaps most of us do not realise that neurosis is very common and takes many forms. For example, a study reported by Eysenck (1977) in his book *You and Neurosis* concluded that between 30 and 35 per cent of the population considered themselves to be suffering from some form of emotional disturbance ('nerves', depression, sleeplessness and 'undue irritability'). One person in three! It seems incredible. In fact most of these cases cannot have been serious, because only 8 per cent, or one in 12, of the population actually sought medical treatment for their neurosis. Nonetheless, one in three means that about 10 million adults at any one time in Britain alone have symptoms of neurosis.

PERSONALITY AND NEUROSIS

There has been a great deal of discussion about the importance of personality in the development of neurosis. First of all, it is not a question of intelligence, since intelligent people are as likely to suffer neurosis as unintelligent people. The discussion really concerns the relationship between neurosis and personality characteristics such as 'emotional stability' and 'extroversion'. Let us look first of all at one of the most common personality classifications in use in psychology, one developed by the German psychologist W. Wundt in the last century. He postulated that every personality type could be described by locating someone's position along two axes of personality – one indicating stability and instability (speed of emotional change), the other indicating extroversion and introversion (strength of emotional expression). This is illustrated by Figure 5/1.

Unstable

- moody
- anxious
- rigid
- sober
- pessimistic
- reserved
- unsociable
- quiet

- touchy
- restless
- aggressive
- excitable
- changeable
- impulsive
- optimistic
- active

Introverted — Extroverted

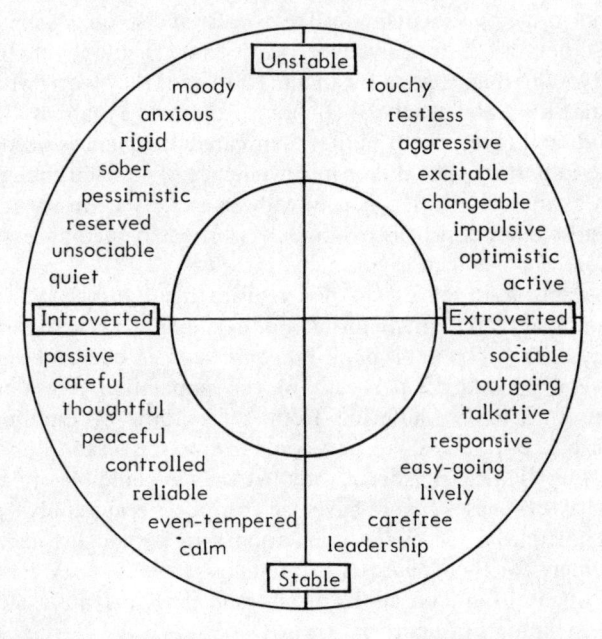

- passive
- careful
- thoughtful
- peaceful
- controlled
- reliable
- even-tempered
- calm

- sociable
- outgoing
- talkative
- responsive
- easy-going
- lively
- carefree
- leadership

Stable

Fig. 5/1 The relationships between different aspects of personality

The 'average' man falls round about the intersection of two axes: he is neither excessively emotional nor extroverted. Other, more distinctly identifiable, personality types can be located anywhere in the four quarters of the circle, according to the degree of extroversion and stability they involve. There is a close relationship between adjacent characteristics within each quarter of the circle, so that adjacent characteristics are often found to occur in the same person. Conversely, the further apart any two personality characteristics are located on the diagram, the less often they are found together. If they are separated by an angle of 90°, there is no correlation between them (in other words, one occurs in a person independently of the other); if they are separated by an angle greater than 90°, they are negatively correlated (they tend not to be found together).

When personality tests are applied to neurotic individuals, they usually score in such a way that their personalities fall into the top left quarter of the circle, i.e. they are emotionally unstable and introverted. This is perhaps what one would intuitively expect, but is there any biological reason why neurosis should be closely linked with instability and introversion?

Firstly, neurosis is (by definition) a condition which involves strong emotional reactions to life events, so the high emotional instability score is not surprising. The brain mechanism which leads to emotional instability is controlled by the functioning of the autonomic nervous system (this is defined in Chapter 1). To some extent, individuals differ in the size of the responses which their autonomic nervous system makes under any set of circumstances – hence, we feel different degrees of fear, anger, and so on. Clearly, neurotic individuals will have a more active autonomic nervous system.

Secondly, extroversion and introversion depend on the level of activity of a higher part of the brain called the cortex which also controls conscious thought. The higher the level of cortical activity, the more introverted one becomes. The interesting aspect of this is that when cortical activity is at a high level for much of the time, as it is in introverts, learning, remembering and conditioning effects are much more marked in an individual.

Thirdly, although we have not yet covered the subject, we shall see that neurosis is frequently a conditioned response. For the moment, conditioning can be regarded as a subconscious learning process: the greater the conditioning, the greater the neuroticism. Two features which an individual must show before he displays strong conditioning are: strong emotional responses, and a high tendency to be conditioned. These two features involve, of course, the emotional instability and introversion referred to above, hence many neurotics fall into the top left quarter of the personality chart.

But what does it mean in practical terms? If the characteristics essential for neuroticism are related to the activity of the autonomic nervous system and cortex, surely our personalities cannot be changed? That assumption would be quite wrong, because we are not born with the activity levels of our brains genetically fixed. In actual fact our genetic make-up can set limits only on the potential extent of our brain activity, a fact which scientists reflect by saying that something like 50 per cent of the variation in personality between individuals is caused by experience and environment.

There are many influences which contribute to your total environment, the most obvious being your home, job, friends, and so on. These may cause you stress, but, as we have already seen, it is possible to avoid stress by changing your beliefs about yourself and the world. And even if you cannot avoid stress, you can lessen its effects by learning to relax. But perhaps the most important influence of all is your own attitude of mind towards neurosis – whether you regard it as inescapable or intolerable, unavoidable or unpleasant. This will be the main factor in how quickly you change – if you want to. In summary, then, brain structure and genetic inheritance only make neurotic problems more or less likely to develop, and whether or not they actually do so depends entirely on your environment. Ultimately, your environment is how you have learnt to see the world and react to it: that is what you can control, and that is what this book is all about.

REFERENCE

Eysenck, H. J. (1977). *You and Neurosis*, p. 31. Maurice Temple Smith, London.

6. Defeating Depression

We all go through periods of unhappiness or sadness in life. Such emotions are a natural reaction to adverse circumstances or events, and usually pass fairly quickly. Depression, on the other hand, involves more persistent feelings of dejection – perhaps even despair. In its worst form, depression affects every aspect of a person's life and may even make him unable to live in a normal way. With a mild depression, a person can live more or less normally, but he or she feels miserable and may not enjoy life very much. Curiously, there are many people who live much of their lives in a state of mild depression and accept this as normal, even to the point of believing that everyone else feels the same way: in fact they simply do not realise that they are depressed. Other people are ashamed to admit that they suffer from depression because they consider it to be a sign of 'weakness'. And many people do not believe they are depressed because they think depression only refers to a serious mental illness. Another group of people are never diagnosed as 'depressed' because physical and emotional problems such as mild but persistent tension and irritability mask the depression itself.

At this point it is appropriate to emphasise two facts. Firstly, depression is extremely common: some estimates suggest that at any one time in Britain alone there are about one million adults between the ages of 20 and 60 suffering from some degree of depression. Secondly, depression can strike at anyone, no matter how clever, happy or normal they may appear to be. It is true that slightly more women than men experience depression, but no-one can be sure they are safe from the problem.

There are three main types of depression:

1. Manic-depressive illness

2. Depressive illness, or endogenous depression
3. Reactive depression

Although manic-depressive illness does not really have a place in a 'self-help' book, a description of the condition is given: anyone who thinks they may be experiencing it should see a doctor.

MANIC-DEPRESSIVE ILLNESS

Typically, periods of 'highs' alternate with 'lows'. During the high or manic phase a person will be frantically active and take on more and more work, which he completes easily, often working 20 hours a day. This apparently boundless energy is matched by an apparent lack of a need to sleep, and over-activity of the intellect as the sufferer dreams up all kinds of new ideas and schemes, most of which are quite impractical. Nevertheless, he declares his intention of seeing them through regardless of criticism. Social pastimes increase dramatically. To take only one example, wild parties at which no-one can get a word in edgeways because of the sufferer's endless chatter are common. Other behaviours such as indiscriminate sexual promiscuity or the senseless spending of money may be more harmful, but the person concerned does not see himself as ill and in need of treatment.

In the depressive phase, matters are quite different. The sufferer seems incapable of even the simplest action – his job, driving his car, any social contact. (This, as we shall see, mirrors the symptoms of depressive illness.) Not all manic-depressives actually show such extreme fluctuations of mood, and sometimes one part of the cycle is much more obvious than the other. Fortunately, the condition responds well to treatment.

You should not automatically assume that everyone who experiences dramatic swings of mood is manic-depressive. Far from it. They may just represent the natural variability of human emotions.

DEPRESSIVE ILLNESS AND REACTIVE DEPRESSION

These two forms of depression have distinctly different causes and cures, even though they may at times appear superficially

DEFEATING DEPRESSION

similar. Depressive illness has a physical basis: it is caused by changes in the chemistry of the brain. (This imbalance can usually be restored to normality with anti-depressant drugs.) Reactive depression, on the other hand, is an extreme emotional response to stressful circumstances or events. In general, reactive depressions do not respond to drugs but can be alleviated by tranquillisers, hypnotherapy, counselling and other forms of psychotherapy. The exception to these broad outlines is that reactive depressions sometimes seem to worsen and take on the characteristics of depressive illness. Below are two lists of the symptoms of these two forms of depression (most people show only some of these symptoms).

A person experiencing depressive illness may:

- feel exhausted and have very little energy, even for the smallest task
- lose interest in his or her work and have great difficulty in running his or her life as before
- feel totally despairing and believe the future is hopeless
- fall asleep easily but wake very early in the morning, at three or four o'clock
- feel terribly depressed in the morning but improve as the day wears on
- feel that his or her emotions are completely uncontrollable
- attempt to explain the depression by referring – wrongly – to 'overwork', 'stress' or some similar problem
- experience a loss of appetite, weight and sex drive to a greater or lesser extent
- be unable to identify any event which might have caused the depression
- show a marked slowing up of thought and activity
- be highly agitated, restless and anxious
- feel extreme guilt about some trivial event perhaps long since past, and relate it to the depression
- experience hallucinations or delusions

Whereas a person experiencing reactive depression may:

- say that he or she feels moody, sad, depressed or unhappy
- have trouble falling asleep but wake at the normal time, although feeling tired and depressed

- experience a swing in the depth of the depression, usually finding that it's worse in the evening or when alone
- feel worse as the day progresses
- be anxious and irritable with associated fears and phobias
- have various personality problems such as a lack of confidence, poor self-esteem, feelings of inferiority or inadequacy (see Chapter 11)
- be less able to think clearly, remember things and concentrate
- experience little or no loss of sex drive (although male impotency as a result of associated personality problems is not uncommon)
- experience little or no loss of appetite or weight (although anxiety may lead to an increase in eating as a source of self-comfort)

Although you might conclude from these lists of symptoms that the two conditions are clearly defined, there has for many years been a great deal of dispute whether they are or not. Perhaps the best way of avoiding this controversy is to adopt the following viewpoint:

... it is not possible to say that the simple reactive depression will be necessarily mild, or the endogenous [i.e., depressive illness] be severe, for they do not follow so simple a pattern ... The mild reactive depressions are [often] placed at one extreme and the severe psychotic depressions at the other end of the spectrum, with moderate and mixed depressions in the middle. This is a convenient way of looking at the problem, but it is in fact an oversimplification. There are indeed relatively benign cases of endogenous depression that would have to be placed at the mild end of the spectrum, which is not, therefore, entirely made up of reactive cases ... The main thing is to recognise the patient is depressed, and if simple listening and advice about obvious problems does not help, then the patient should be referred to a doctor competent to make an accurate diagnosis and give the proper treatment. (Watts, 1973.)

Of course, anyone who thinks he or she has a depressive illness should see a doctor, for, as should now be clear, depressive illness is a medical problem not suited to self-help treatments. However, it may be helpful to discuss certain aspects of the condition in more detail.

DEPRESSIVE ILLNESS

The most obvious question about this subject is: 'What causes a depressive illness?' To answer this, you need to understand a little about the working of the brain.

The reward centre, or emotional control centre, is the part of the brain that produces the feelings of satisfaction or pleasure which we experience when we have completed some action. These feelings act as our incentive to repeat that action. Under certain conditions, however, the reward centre can, as it were, 'switch off', and when this happens, one feels low or depressed all the time. This is a physical illness in the sense that a part of the body has stopped functioning as it should. But why does this happen?

Extreme mental and physical fatigue is a common cause of depressive illness. For example, a businessman who works long hours under great pressure for many years while he builds up his business runs the risk of anxiety, worry, chronic fatigue and eventually depression. Few people, in fact, could take on such a demanding role without eventually suffering for it.

There are other reasons why the activity of the brain's reward centre sometimes changes. Those people who experience depressive illness after surgery, for example, may have a brain which is very sensitive to the chemical action of the anaesthetic.

Depressive illness which occurs during adolescence, after childbirth or at the menopause may be associated with natural hormonal fluctuations in an individual's body. Indeed, one of the most common forms of depression is postnatal depression. Many women seem to experience a low mood for at least a short period after childbirth, but this is comparatively trivial in comparison to the serious and persistent depression which develops in a few women. This condition is marked by tearfulness, uncontrollable crying or mood swings at the least provocation, and the other symptoms listed earlier.

Sometimes depressive illness seems to develop from the stress-induced reactive depression; it is as though there is a limit to the amount of stress which the reward centre can take before it 'switches off'.

All cases of depressive illness should be referred to professional help as soon as possible.

UNDERSTANDING REACTIVE DEPRESSION

Ultimately, all reactive depression is a reaction to stress. In this section, we shall offer some suggestions about the nature of the connection between stress and depression. In trying to understand this question, we need to keep one particular point firmly in mind: this form of depression is not controlled by genetic inheritance. It is in fact a combination of life events and life experience (i.e. what we learn and what happens to us) that determines whether or not we become depressed.

Reactive depression can be divided into two broad categories: *authentic depression* and *manipulative depression*. A manipulative depression seems to be a conscious or subconscious psychological ploy to manipulate the attitudes and behaviour of other people, whereas an authentic depression is a 'genuine' reaction to stressful life events. (But do note that all depressions are just as genuine to the person suffering them, and if a depressed person is told to 'snap out of it' by somebody with little understanding of the problem, he will only feel more wretched and miserable. For, if he could 'snap out of it', he would have done so long ago. And even if a person is subconsciously choosing to be depressed for some ulterior motive, he wouldn't be that way if he knew how to do something constructive about his problem.)

AUTHENTIC DEPRESSION

This term is intended to suggest that a person is caught up in circumstances which seem so stressful that he or she becomes overwhelmed with depression. Let us now examine how and why this can happen. Our discussion falls naturally into several sections.

1. Loss events and separation

Consider a girl who is deeply in love with her boy friend. If he decides to end their relationship, she will naturally be very upset and could react in a variety of ways. She may be unhappy for a while, but continue to live normally; she may be deeply unhappy and find that she obtains less satisfaction from her life and work; or she may become severely depressed. Now, this example represents a whole area of life experiences which can be grouped under the heading 'loss events'.

A loss event in adult life is one which involves the removal of something we value from our lives. Thus, typical examples of loss events include:

- the death of a spouse
- the ending of a relationship
- the loss of a job, family, friends, and perhaps even valued objects
- moving home to a new area
- the family leaving home

and so on. No doubt you can think of many more.

There is a body of opinion which suggests that we react to this type of event with depression if we were 'sensitised' to it during childhood. In other words, if an emotional or physical loss in childhood causes depression, situations which have some similarity later in life will evoke the same depressive response. To understand this idea more clearly, we need to consider the sort of events which might be particularly significant to a child.

One major cause of emotional problems during childhood is the breaking of the bonds between a child and its parents. A child's relationships with its parents are the first and most important interactions which it establishes with anyone else. Indeed, we now know that a strong bond between mother and child is normally established immediately after birth through feeding, touching, smiling, talking and so forth. Should this bond be broken (for example, through separation caused by illness or death) the child may respond to other losses later in life with anxiety and depression.

Of course, children are capable of interpreting even the most insignificant separation or loss events as being of major importance. For example, a child whose father is away for weeks at a time may think that the separation means his father does not love him. Even the disappearance of any much loved object such as a pet or toy can cause a great sense of loss.

It has been suggested (Parker, 1978) that disruption (rather than complete breakage) of the bonds between parents and children can also contribute to depression in adulthood. He has described two broad categories of disruption: *underbonding* and *overbonding*.

2. Underbonding and overbonding

Underbonding implies that a child's parents fail to provide adequate love, affection, attention or praise. This can happen if the parents are habitually depressed and withdrawn. Alternatively, they may deliberately ignore, denigrate, reject or criticise the child to a greater or lesser extent. But whatever the cause, a child readily comes to believe what he is told or what he deduces from his parents' lack of interest in him: that he is worthless, insignificant, foolish and incompetent. (That is an extreme case, but the same principles are at work in both mild and serious cases of underbonding.)

Personality characteristics of people with this sort of upbringing may include introversion; minimal independence; lack of assertive and aggressive behaviour; habitual pessimism about the world, life, the future and relationships. It is said that people like this are over-sensitive to the opinions of others and therefore experience considerable anxiety. They also have a low self-esteem and hold many negative expectations about life. Now, when a person holds many negative expectations about himself and his life, some of them will inevitably be fulfilled. When this happens, the individual thinks his or her pessimism is justified, and so he or she sinks deeper into depression even if the event which provokes this reaction is really quite trivial. (Incidentally, this principle is probably true for specific areas of life as well, which may explain why one sometimes reacts very emotionally to an event which is objectively unimportant. The implication is that somehow one was sensitised to that kind of event during childhood.)

Overbonding, in contrast, implies an excessive or unusual involvement of (generally) the mother in her children's lives. A mother may develop an unusually close relationship with a child for various reasons. For example, she may have greatly desired a child but failed to conceive until late in life, or she may herself have been deprived of love during her childhood. In any event, she becomes noticeably overprotective and inhibits the development of normal independence in her child. Such children may have a normal level of self-esteem, but subconsciously they tend to believe that it is tied to this one relationship, so that separation produces anxiety and depression. On a more general level, Parker suggests that overbonding produces a person who tends to become dependent on other people later in life. And, as we explained earlier, a person who is dependent on someone else in a relationship will probably become depressed when that relationship ends.

As you might expect there appears to be a clear connection between parental overprotectiveness and normal feelings of sadness and unhappiness. The clear implication of this is that an overprotective parent prevents his or her child from learning how to cope with life's difficulties. Overbonding is complicated by the fact that an 'overbonded child' often has an externalised self-esteem: this means that he or she regards criticism or praise of his actions as criticism or praise of him as a person, an attitude which develops when one's parents make remarks like 'We don't love you when you do that', rather than 'We love you but we don't like you to do that.' To some extent we all experience this problem of externalised self-esteem; we should remember that criticism of one's actions is not the same as criticism of one as a person.

3. *Learned helplessness*

Psychologists have suggested that human depression is a form of learned helplessness. This is a simple idea: if your actions, either in childhood or adulthood, do not influence the people and the world around you, then you come to believe that you cannot exert any control over what happens to you. It is easy to see how such a belief could produce feelings of depression and despair. Obviously a child who is ignored by his parents is likely to develop these feelings, and we may suppose that an adult who has difficulty in being assertive is also likely to develop this particular problem. In any event, learned helplessness is a feeling of depression and a belief that everything is beyond your control which occurs in stressful circumstances.

4. *The repression of anger*

There are other ways in which parents may make their children more likely to suffer depression in adult life, even within the framework of a 'normal' childhood. For example, some parents punish their child's displays of anger or aggression so severely that the child becomes inhibited from consciously accepting or displaying his aggressive urges. Up to a point, of course, children do have to be restrained from self-indulgent behaviour, otherwise they might not conform to socially acceptable standards. But if this is taken to extremes, the child develops into an adult who represses all his angry and aggressive feelings. Now, many psychiatrists and psychologists believe that repressed anger is a major cause of depression and anxiety. The reasoning is that if you don't express your anger, it must inevitably be turned inwards against yourself and so become the cause of much depression. One might expect that at least some depressed people who were encouraged to express anger would experience a lessening of their depression; this does indeed seem to be the case.

5. *Learning by imitation*

A child develops much of its behaviour and a large proportion of its thoughts, feelings and attitudes by watching and imitating its parents. Thus, if a child sees his parents get depressed at every setback or obstacle in life, as an adult he may himself react in a similar way to stressful events.

As a general rule, therefore, we can say that the wide variation in individual childhood experience is a factor of great importance in determining a person's depressive tendency later in life. In practice this means that some people will never experience depression, some people will respond to trivial stress with depression, and some will only feel depressed after they have experienced many very stressful events.

6. *Stressful events in adulthood*

There are many cases of stress-related depression which have no obvious connection with childhood influences. Two very common examples are depression which develops after some personal success (often, but not always, in one's employment) and depression in an unhappy marriage.

You may think it strange that success and achievement can induce depression, but there is no doubt that this does sometimes happen. Why should this be so? You may yourself have worked towards some goal, putting time and effort into reaching it, only to feel a sense of anticlimax and emptiness when you did so. The obvious implication of this is that our objectives may be less fulfilling in reality than in our imagination. Consider a man who achieves his personal target of managing director. He may suddenly realise that his life has become strangely 'empty', with nothing to work for and nothing to look forward to. Perhaps he realises that he is isolated from his wife and family because he has paid more attention to his business than his home. Perhaps he discovers that he has been used by 'friends' who thought he might be able to help with their careers or promotion. Perhaps even his marriage was based on his wife's appreciation of his ambition and ability rather than his personality. To sum up, he may become depressed because he sees himself as having succeeded in business but failed in some other areas of life. This will be made worse if he realises that those other areas of life actually mean more to him than his managing directorship.

Depression in marriage is very common, a fact which is not surprising since there can be more sources of stress in marriage than in any other relationship. To take only one example, some people marry because one partner fulfils a need in the other. Such a marriage is fine for as long as the partners maintain the same relationship, but the trouble is that such interactions tend not to last very long. A classic example is the man who marries at the start of his career when he needs a wife who can skimp and save, bring up the children and run a house on a low income. Later, he moves into top management and wants a wife who can act as a perfect host, converse on an equal level with his colleagues' wives and support his ambitions. If his wife cannot or will not adapt to this role, the conflicts that arise could cause her to become depressed. In addition, the husband may deliberately undermine his wife's self-esteem with hurtful remarks about her ability, appearance and attitudes, and so make her feel even more depressed. If the couple go on living with this relationship, the situation can only get worse.

Another common example is the marriage where the husband wants his wife to look after him as his mother used to. This rather immature 'parent-child' relationship is all very well as long as both husband and wife stick to their defined roles, but as soon as one of them begins to move away from his or her role, trouble is not only likely – it is almost certain.

There are so many experiences and events which can cause depression that it is only possible to list some of the more common ones:

- the conflict in adolescence between dependency on one's parents and a desire to break away from them
- the financial pressures and loss of self-respect which can result from unemployment
- the isolating and restricting effects of shyness
- the stress of loneliness
- an inability to achieve personal goals
- when the demands of employment exceed one's ability to cope
- moving from a familiar environment to a strange one
- the type of loss events listed earlier (p. 85)
- when someone on whom you are dependent for your emotional well-being leaves you
- an inability to obtain sexual fulfilment or other sexual worries
- periods of ill-health
- during the period after the birth of her baby, when a mother finds that her romantic notions of motherhood are dispelled by feeding, clothing, changing the baby's clothes, and sleepless nights
- an unhappy home environment (see below)

The depressogenic environment

As we implied above, the stress of human relationships can be a major cause of depression. A depressogenic environment has been described as one in which 'thousands of verbal and non-verbal exchanges take place daily . . . and stir up in the vulnerable individual a loss of self-esteem, guilt, inexpressible anger and a sense of not being understood' (Flach, 1975). Here are some examples of the ways in which some members of a family may keep others depressed:

Keeping an individual from finding some degree of independence, while one or several members of the family maintain control

Stirring up separation anxiety; that is, encouraging a dependency that convinces the more dependent member that he cannot possibly survive without their emotional support

Delivering ambivalent messages that undermine self-esteem and at the same time block legitimate self-defence, such as 'I love you, in spite of the kind of person you are'

Repeatedly provoking guilt by making the other person feel responsible, regardless of the facts

Misinterpreting intentions and motives so that the more insecure member begins to doubt his own perceptions, even though they are more accurate

Contaminating family interactions with a competitiveness that stems from envy and jealousy

Providing a monotonous, unstimulating environment that resists any effort to introduce humour, spontaneity, and joy

Refusing to permit any open show of emotion, and in particular healthy reactions of anger

Using a chronic state of depression to express anger indirectly, making others feel helpless, guilty and confused in the process

Blocking open and direct communication

Depression and anxiety

Depression and anxiety frequently occur together. This is not surprising, for they can be thought of as two extremes of a spectrum of possible responses to stress. Depression is a direct result of stresses caused by circumstances which exist now, or events which have happened in the past; anxiety, on the other hand, can take the form of fearfulness about what might happen in the future.

Quite often, anxiety is 'free-floating', that is, not focused on anything in particular. However, it can readily focus on all sorts of common problems: financial difficulties, health problems, the state of the world, crime in the streets – the list is endless. Irrational worries like these produce considerable anxiety, so that a depressed person may therefore find that his already dreadful burden of depression is increased by extreme anxiety about all sorts of problems which seem all too real to him.

Anxiety makes the experience of depression even more unpleasant. Sometimes it is so intense that it disguises depression. We shall look at anxiety in more detail in Chapter 7, so it would be out of place to discuss it here. You should, however, note that you can combine treatment for feelings of anxiety and depression.

Depression as a cause of further stress

Besides being caused by stress, depression may act as a source of further stress and so can produce tension, anxiety, irritability, guilt and psychosomatic illness. Sometimes these problems actually mask the depression itself. In such circumstances, a useful guide to depression is predominant feelings of inadequacy, inferiority, a poor self-esteem and a lack of confidence.

Depression and the people around you

There can hardly be a single depressed person who hasn't heard one of these remarks:

'Pull yourself together.'
'What's wrong with you?'
'Why are you looking like that?'
'You owe it to us to be cheerful.'
'You've got nothing to be depressed about.'
'You must fight this, and not give in to it.'

Such remarks are hurtful. They usually deepen a depression because the sufferer's sense of injustice is increased or because he feels even more guilty about 'letting people down'. However, these remarks are usually made out of a sense of helplessness and ignorance because family and friends don't know what they can do to help a depressed person. Some books which may be useful will be found in the list of Further Reading on page 163.

MANIPULATIVE DEPRESSION

Manipulative depression is not an authentic reaction to stress, but a conscious or subconscious behaviour pattern which is designed to elicit a particular attitude or behaviour from another person. However, this does not mean that someone who displays this kind of behaviour is deliberately *choosing* to be depressed. Most often, this kind of behaviour occurs simply because a person learnt during childhood that acting sulkily or depressed was enough to produce attention and sympathy from his or her parents. Later in life, that person may still display the same pattern of behaviour. Such a learning process is subconsciously determined, so the person concerned probably does not even realise what he or she is doing. For example, a girl who watches her mother successfully and continually manipulating her father by means of 'moods', 'depressions', and so on, is herself likely to display a similar pattern of behaviour later in life.

Consider once again the case of a girl whose boy friend ends their relationship. She may 'replay' childhood patterns of behaviour as depression or sulking. But the crucial difference between this and authentic depression is that the sympathy she receives is actually a 'reward' for the depression. For example, one old woman used depressive behaviour to manipulate the behaviour of her adult son and daughter, who were still living with her. Whenever anything threatened the stability of this situation, the old woman showed unexplained and mysterious signs of illness: her doctor persuaded the daughter to take a holiday – her first for many years. Half-way through, the old woman fell 'ill' and instructed her son to have the police bring the daughter home. Matters went on like this for some years until she died. In many such cases, this behaviour is depressive and begins when the husband dies, leaving a dreadful gap in the widow's life. The ill-health is an obvious strategy for gaining attention.

Treatment of a depression like this is not easy. First of all, one has to overcome the 'self-destructive', subconscious programming that makes the person in question behave as he or she does. One woman in a treatment group was asked under hypnosis: 'How much do you need your illness to obtain your husband's sympathy?' Without thinking, she replied: 'About 90 per cent.' Later she phoned to deny it. 'I don't know why I said it,' she told her therapist; 'it isn't true.' Needless to say, she did not recover from her depression.

WHAT YOU CAN DO ABOUT STRESS-INDUCED DEPRESSION

Besides actually treating your depression with one or other of the self-hypnosis techniques, you should try to lessen the stress which caused it in the first place. You can do this through a process of changing your beliefs and attitudes as we described in Chapters 1 and 2, but this is often a slow and lengthy business, and you may therefore wish to obtain help in dealing with stressful situations from professional counsellors or advice centres. But unless you are guided by your doctor, you need to be careful in selecting people to help with physical, sexual or emotional problems. Discrimination is also necessary when you are seeking advice on vocational guidance and other life problems. You should ensure that the agency or person you approach is a member of an established organization, and also that the individuals with whom you deal have real experience of the problem (see pages 165–6 for some useful addresses).

Self-hypnosis

If you use the *tape recorder technique*, use the normal Stage 1 induction process and the standard Stage 3 coming-out procedure. Suggestions for Stage 2, the treatment stage, could include:

i) Treatment for depression, as follows:
Your depression is troubling you less and less often, less and less severely all the time now, and very soon now it will have gone away completely. The feelings of depression which trouble you are occurring less and less often. You are becoming more relaxed and cheerful; each day brings about an improvement in your own feelings and your attitude to life. Depression is caused by stress, and as you learn to relax and cope with stress, feelings of depression trouble you less and less. This treatment provides complete rest for your mind and body so that feelings of stress and tension are going away more and more. You are becoming more

calm and relaxed. And because you are more calm and relaxed, your enjoyment of life will increase. Your ability to get on with people is also improving all the time. This is because feelings of depression are troubling you less and less often, less and less severely all the time now.

In addition, as you feel necessary:
ii) Suggestions to reduce anxiety, fears and worries (see pp. 107–8).
iii) Suggestions to use the five deep breaths to counteract physical and mental tension (see p. 65 and p. 67).
iv) Suggestions to lessen feelings of inferiority or to increase self-confidence (see Chapter 11).
v) Suggestions to deal with any other personal problem (see p. 116 for an example of this).

We strongly suggest that you incorporate the five deep breaths as a trigger to help you relax in moments of increased tension, unhappiness, anxiety and depression.

Autosuggestion can also be used for depression. The method was described in Chapter 4. If you use this technique, keep your suggestions simple, for example:

'Every day I am feeling more calm, relaxed, confident and cheerful.'

'Every day, feelings of depression are troubling me less and less often, less and less severely.'

REFERENCES

Flach, F. (1975). *The Secret Strength of Depression*, pp. 138–9. Angus and Robertson, London.

Parker, G. (1978). *The Bonds of Depression*. Angus and Robertson, London.

Watts, C. A. H. (1973). *Depression: The Blue Plague*, pp. 30–1. Priory Press, London.

7. What is Anxiety?

Anxiety is an emotional state which combines unpleasant thoughts and feelings with bodily changes controlled by the autonomic nervous system. (The autonomic nervous system is explained in Chapter 1.)

Anxiety states, unlike that definition, are not simple and straightforward. They take many forms; they have many causes; they vary in both intensity and duration; and, lastly, the exact combination of emotional and physical symptoms involved varies from person to person. To simplify this discussion, we have divided them into separate categories.

NERVOUSNESS AND SOCIAL, SEXUAL, LIFE AND WORK ANXIETIES

These are short-term anxiety states which we all experience from time to time. For example, we tend to use the word *nervousness* to refer to the moderate amount of anxiety which we feel in situations where failure or poor performance could have personally unpleasant consequences.

Examples of this include the nervousness of an actor before his performance, a public speaker before he delivers his address and a sportsman before he plays his match. As we explained in Chapter 1, the mental and physical arousal associated with such events may actually help to improve one's performance. But many people find that they are over-aroused in particular social, sexual, life or work situations.

If you are one of these people, you will not need to be told that this excessive nervousness or *social anxiety* is completely unhelpful. First of all, it reduces your ability to think clearly and

WHAT IS ANXIETY?

to concentrate, instead filling your mind with confused and worried thoughts. Then, as it increases in intensity, it begins to affect your body. Your palms may sweat, your heart may pound, your stomach may churn, your mouth go dry, your face burn with embarrassment (not to mention other more inconvenient problems). Although you may know you really have nothing to fear, your emotions seem to overpower your reason. No matter how important it is for you to speak confidently, express yourself clearly, or demonstrate your ability, your confidence and ability are undermined by your anxiety. Small wonder, then, that the victim of anxiety often feels and looks ridiculous. In Chapter 11, we offer some suggestions as to why one sometimes experiences an unreasonable and inappropriate feeling of anxiety before and during events which pose no objective threat. (For example: when talking to a group of colleagues, when meeting people for the first time, when waiting for friends to call, when going to a party, when making love, when speaking on the telephone, and so on.) We also discuss feelings of inferiority, poor self-esteem, lack of confidence and the question of self-image because such problems often form a background to social anxiety. And in Chapter 8 we offer some advice on coping with feelings of anxiety as they occur.

FEARS AND PHOBIAS

Perhaps, strictly speaking, the word *fear* should only be used to describe the very intense emotional response which we sometimes feel in objectively dangerous or frightening situations. (For example, when people in a burning building become paralysed in terror, we know that their main emotion is fear.) However, fear has come to imply a much wider range of feelings of anxiety and worry. To take but one example, you might say of a shy person: 'He has a fear of meeting people.' And that is how we shall use the word later in this book.

Fear sometimes develops when there is no rational explanation for it. If a person says that he or she is afraid of dogs or cats, flying or high places, enclosed or open spaces, he may well have a *phobia*. This is an irrational (but real) fear of an object, event, place or situation. Phobic fear, or more correctly phobic anxiety, is the emotional response of a phobic person to the object of his phobia.

There are both simple and complex phobias. As we shall see, one of the most common (agoraphobia, the fear of open or crowded places) is also one of the most complicated. Phobias are discussed in Chapter 9.

PERSISTENT ANXIETY AND ANXIETY ATTACKS

So far we have considered what are obviously short-term anxiety states. But sometimes a person feels anxious or 'nervous' for much – or even all – of the time. He may have a tense posture, strained facial expression, jerky movements; he may complain of pains in his body or headaches; he may have an upset stomach and perspiring hands; he feels nervous and his hands may tremble; and he often claims a feeling of danger or impending catastrophe, although he does not know what he fears. Even at moderate levels of anxiety, rational thoughts may be replaced by irrational worries, or a person may become constantly apprehensive with a vague feeling of threat hanging over him. Freud was the first to recognise this condition, and called it 'free floating anxiety'. We have called it *persistent anxiety* to emphasise the contrast with anxiety felt in specific situations. It is explained in Chapter 8.

Occasionally, people experience a short-lived but intense *anxiety attack*. Sometimes these attacks occur 'out of the blue', but more often they occur in a person who is fairly anxious anyway. They represent an exaggerated response by the nervous system to mild stimuli. Sometimes the response is so extreme that no more than a disturbing thought causes marked feelings of anxiety, and in the worst cases a stimulus so insignificant that it cannot even be identified causes a major attack of panic. This can be very alarming, because all the symptoms of anxiety listed above may occur at once and reduce the person concerned to total confusion. These attacks play a major part in agoraphobia. We shall see what can be done about them in Chapter 8.

WORRIED THINKING

It has been said that the basis of all anxiety is worried thinking (see Chapter 10). People frequently worry about strange things when they are suffering from anxiety.

Before we go on to discuss each of these anxiety-related problems in more detail, we need to outline some points which are relevant to all forms of anxiety. These include the effects of anxiety, and the different ways in which anxiety can develop.

THE EFFECTS OF ANXIETY

We need not dwell on the effects of anxiety, for they will be obvious enough to people who are prone to anxiety. Besides the list of symptoms on pages 96–7, they include:

- feelings of irritability, depression, guilt and hostility
- a tendency to introspection, self-criticism and negative thoughts
- excessive dependency on other people
- an inability to perform well in stressful situations such as examinations or interviews
- a susceptibility to phobias and irrational worry
- a tendency to psychosomatic illness and worries about health
- a decrease in one's ability to function efficiently in life and to cope with everyday problems

THE CAUSES OF ANXIETY STATES

Anxiety is probably the most common human reaction to stress. This is not surprising, for the bodily changes associated with anxiety are very similar to those involved in our response to stress. (These changes are, of course, caused by increased activity of the autonomic nervous system. This, and the nature of stress, are explained in Chapter 1.) However, it is the emotional and cognitive components of anxiety which allow us to distinguish between human reaction to stress in general and anxiety in particular.

Although the anxiety we feel may well be caused by some stressful event or situation, it must be obvious even to the most unskilled student of human nature that different people respond to the same stressful event in very different ways. These individual variations have been ascribed to anxiety traits in the human personality.

ANXIETY TRAITS

The term 'anxiety trait' refers to the personality trait which determines the frequency and severity with which an individual experiences anxiety states over a long period of time. A person high in trait anxiety worries much more than one low in trait anxiety. He sees the world as a more threatening place and responds to his perceptions of threat with greater anxiety, and, if he is subjected to stress for a long time, he may eventually become continuously aroused.

To some extent, anxiety traits are determined genetically. Another factor of great importance must be the influence of one's parents during childhood, because they teach one how to respond to life events. And there is no doubt that the type of negative parent–child relationships described in Chapter 6 predispose an individual to be anxious in later life. This is because an insecure individual who is unsure of his own self-worth will tend to feel apprehensive about his relationships with the world in general and other people in particular. Also it is quite likely that negative experiences in one's early schooldays contribute to trait anxiety. However, we do not wish to imply that every anxious person must have had an unhappy childhood, for that would clearly be an over-generalisation.

REPRESSION AND CONDITIONING

In Chapter 1 we explained the mechanism of repression. To recap very briefly, repression involves the suppression of unpleasant or unacceptable thoughts, feelings and emotions into the subconscious mind, in an attempt to stop them acting as a source of psychological distress or discomfort.

It is a basic tenet of Freudian psychology that repression is the

WHAT IS ANXIETY?

mechanism of neurotic anxiety (that is, any form of anxiety not caused by an objective danger or threat). The ways in which repression is able to cause specific forms of anxiety will become clear in later chapters, and for the moment we need only note that individuals with marked anxiety traits may be especially vulnerable to the experience of anxiety precipitated by a breakdown in repression.

Freudian psychology was dominant for many years. But when *behavioural psychology* began to develop, it was realised that anxiety states could be treated without reference to repressed material. In fact, behavioural psychology emphasises that anxiety is a behaviour pattern which is maintained through a learning or *conditioning* process, an idea which we shall now examine in more detail.

Our first example of a conditioning process is one which has been described many times in the non-scientific literature. It is the famous case of the Russian scientist Pavlov and his dogs. Pavlov showed that whereas a dog responds to the sight of food by salivating, naturally enough there is no such response to the sound of a bell. But if you put the bell and food together often enough, the dogs will begin to salivate at the sound of the bell alone: in other words, they will be 'conditioned' to expect food when the bell sounds. The sight of food and the natural salivation are called the unconditioned stimulus and response respectively; not unexpectedly, the bell and subsequent salivation are called the conditioned stimulus and response respectively.

Our second example of conditioning illustrates how the process may play a part in the development of anxiety problems. In the early years of this century, a pioneer behavioural scientist, J. B. Watson, conducted some experiments on a nine-month-old baby boy. First of all, he presented a variety of white furry objects, including a rabbit, a white rat, a fur coat and cotton-wool, to the boy and allowed him to touch them. None of these made the boy cry, nor did he show any fear. A gong was then positioned so that the boy could not see it and was struck sharply several times until the boy cried with fear each time he heard it. Subsequently the white rat was presented as the gong was struck, and the boy naturally cried with fear. Next time the rat alone was offered to him without any accompanying noise, the effect was dramatic: the boy cried violently and crawled away. Remember that previously he had played with the rat and shown no fear. In other words, his fear of the gong had been transferred to the sight of the rat. Interestingly, the boy afterwards responded with fear to the sight of any other white furry object: his anxiety had *generalised*.

Watson suggested that we can all be conditioned in childhood by experiencing fear or anxiety in a particular situation, and that afterwards, similar situations will elicit similar feelings of anxiety and fear. And because of the generalisation effect, stimuli rather different to the original one may also cause us to feel fear or anxiety.

Conditioning does not only occur during childhood. We can develop a conditioned anxiety response at any time during our lives. The idea comes down to this: if you feel anxious and aroused in a particular situation, similar situations in the future will also make you feel anxious. And because conditioning is a subconscious process, it makes no difference that your rational conscious mind tells you there is nothing to fear.

Anxiety is unpleasant. There is no doubt about that. And that is why conditioning is so effective. Suppose you are nervous at a social gathering and the anxiety you feel makes you want to get away. Doing so will make you feel much better, but next time you are in the same sort of situation, the anxiety may return. Your desire to 'escape' may be even stronger, and the sense of relief which escape produces will also be more powerful. Eventually you simply avoid the anxiety-making situation altogether. Thus, cat phobics avoid cats, agoraphobics avoid crowded spaces, shy people avoid social contact, and so on. Obviously this sort of behaviour can – for a while – make you feel much better. But by avoiding the cause of your anxiety, you are effectively preventing a reversal of the conditioning process from taking place.

To understand this, consider once again the dogs which have been conditioned to salivate at the sound of a bell. If they hear the bell repeatedly, with no food being presented, they learn that the stimulus is no longer associated with food and eventually the salivation ceases. Of course, such 'extinction' of response can only occur if the subject can see and hear the conditioned stimulus. But, as we have explained, anxious people tend to avoid the source of their anxiety, and because they never confront it, extinction cannot occur.

Conditioning is under the control of the subconscious mind. The conscious mind cannot affect the subconscious or its conditioned responses, so we have the bizarre situation where, say, a woman phobic about cats knows full well that her fear of cats is quite absurd and irrational, but no amount of conscious effort will change the situation.

Conditioning takes place most readily when a person is highly aroused. Therefore a person under stress, who is highly aroused, is predisposed to develop conditioned anxiety responses. Here is an example reported by H. J. Eysenck (1977) which illustrates these ideas very clearly. It concerns a man who experienced anxiety and impotence during sexual relationships with his wife, although he admitted that he only had the problem at home in his own bedroom. It transpired that several years earlier, he had had an affair with another woman. One day her husband had caught him and beaten him rather severely; the bizarre aspect of the matter was that the wallpaper in his own and his lover's bedroom was exactly the same. Each time he tried to make love with his wife, the wallpaper in his own bedroom served as a reminder of the beating, and the anxiety which this produced made him impotent!

We now turn our attention to specific anxiety-related problems, and discuss ways of identifying and dealing with the problems involved.

REFERENCE

Eysenck, H. J. (1977). *You and Neurosis*, p. 69. Maurice Temple Smith, London.

8. How to Control Your Anxiety

This chapter is divided into two parts. In the first part, we examine in more detail the origin and development of what we have called persistent anxiety. In the second part, we describe some techniques designed to help you cope effectively with those less prolonged feelings of anxiety which we all experience in certain specific situations. These techniques are also helpful if you experience attacks of anxiety, but don't know why.

I: UNDERSTANDING AND COPING WITH PERSISTENT ANXIETY

Persistent anxiety states vary in both intensity and duration. Thus, they may involve nothing more than mild muscle tension, headaches, an upset digestion, or something similar, together with a tendency to think anxious and worried thoughts. On the other hand, they can produce much more marked physical effects, especially tension of the neck, back and stomach muscles, and, perhaps most distressing of all, a vague and nonspecific feeling of impending threat or catastrophe. If anxiety continues at a high level for any length of time, a person finds that relaxation and sleep become difficult, and may also develop restless repetitive movements of the body such as finger-tapping.

A person who lives with anxiety like this is physically and emotionally aroused. His emotional responses are therefore exaggerated. For example, he may explode with irritation at any minor annoyance or frustration, and his body may respond to any small shock or startle by producing a surge of adrenalin which starts his heart racing. These responses can be so alarming that he begins to worry about the way he feels. Such worries in themselves contribute to still greater arousal, and in some cases this spiral of increasing anxiety very quickly leads to near panic. But what makes a person become continually aroused?

Anxiety is, of course, caused by stress, and so, as you might expect, persistent anxiety is often caused by persistent or recurrent stress of one sort or another. In fact it is not hard to think of the kind of unpleasant or difficult lifestyles and situations which could act as a source of persistent stress. Although we have already mentioned several examples of such situations in earlier chapters of this book, they are worth repeating once again. For example, a man who dislikes his job but feels he cannot resign because his family needs the security of his employment will experience the stress of many conflicting thoughts and emotions. First and foremost, his desire to abandon his job conflicts with his family's need for financial security. This might in turn produce a conflict between his love for his wife and children and his feelings of resentment about the fact that they are dependent on him. It is also possible that he perceives himself as a 'failure' because he is forced to fulfil a role which he dislikes. You may be able to think of other possible sources of conflict.

Here are some other examples of anxiety-making situations:

- resentments, dependency, hostility or incompatibility between two people in a relationship which they believe they 'cannot' give up
- family conflicts and environment like those described on page 91
- pressures from the behaviour of family members, for example from the behaviour of children at adolescence
- excessive responsibility at work, leading to the worries 'Can I cope?' and 'What will happen if I can't?'
- sudden shock or extreme stress such as a difficult childbirth or a severe illness
- persistent worry about one's health, financial situation, and so on

As explained earlier, not everyone reacts to stress with anxiety. Individual differences in personality are a factor of major importance here; so too is an individual's tendency to worry (see Chapter 10).

Some psychologists have drawn attention to the importance of repressed thoughts, feelings and emotions as a cause of anxiety, and one can indeed often see a connection between repressed thoughts and feelings and a person's anxiety. Take the case of Jane, a middle-aged woman whose husband simply walked out on her with no warning of any kind, so that she suddenly found herself with no income, a house and family to look after, and responsibility for matters she had not even thought about in years. She returned to work but gradually developed persistent anxiety, perhaps because she could not consciously admit the fact that she was worried – worried about money, herself, her family and her friends. The release came one day when she broke down and shouted: 'I'm frightened!' This was the point at which for some reason she had been able to identify and get in touch with the emotions and problems underlying her surface anxiety. In this case, these underlying emotions were primarily ones of fear, doubt and anxiety, but there is evidence that the repression of feelings of aggression and anger can also produce anxiety.

Even if you can't identify the cause of your anxiety, you can still use the techniques described below to lessen its effects. Usually, however, you will have at least a vague idea of what lies behind your anxiety. Careful self-analysis and exploration of your thoughts and feelings can help to uncover more and more of that material. You may also wish to refer to our comments on page 71 about the use of self-hypnosis to uncover repressed thoughts and feelings. Another useful point to remember is that persistent anxiety involves a high level of emotional arousal, so learning to relax can be of considerable benefit. This will lower your overall level of arousal and anxiety, and also tend to reduce the anxiety response you feel in specific situations.

SELF-HELP METHODS OF COPING WITH PERSISTENT ANXIETY

You can reduce persistent anxiety by:

1. *Lessening the stress which causes it*. We described how you can reduce stress by changing your attitudes and beliefs

HOW TO CONTROL YOUR ANXIETY

about the world, your life and yourself in Chapters 1 and 2. Sometimes professional help is useful in this process (see p. 94).

2. *Changing your way of thinking and organising your life.* If your anxiety is associated with a tendency on your part to worry excessively, you should perhaps try to change your mental attitude to events and how they affect you (see Chapter 10). But in the short term, you may be able to help yourself to control feelings of anxiety by running your life more efficiently. This is because anxiety often makes you feel that you are 'going round in circles and getting nowhere'. For example, housewives find that they cannot run their homes as they used to and businessmen find that they become tied up in trivial matters while the important ones go unattended. In general, though, men experience this particular aspect of anxiety less than women because they usually have a daily routine which 'holds things together' for them. And therein lies the clue to dealing with the problem, for careful thought and planning – such as establishing a list of priorities and then working methodically through them, ignoring each item until the one before has been completed – goes a long way to reducing the vicious circle of: *anxiety* produces *inefficiency* which means *less work is completed* which makes *you worry about what remains to be done* which in turn causes *more anxiety*.

3. *Self-hypnosis.* If your anxiety is very severe, you can obtain help and advice from your GP, but you can also do much to help yourself with the methods described in Chapter 4. Here we shall specifically consider the *tape recorder technique*. To apply this technique to anxiety, use the standard Stage 1 induction system and the normal Stage 3 'coming out' procedure. Stage 2 should include suggestions for anxiety something like these:

> Feelings of anxiety are troubling you less and less often, less and less severely all the time now. As you learn to relax more easily and quickly when you use this technique, so all feelings of tension and anxiety are going away. You are becoming more relaxed and calm throughout your entire day, feeling less and less anxious all the time, during

your social, family and business life. Worried thoughts and feelings are also troubling you less and less often, less and less severely all the time now, and very soon now they will have gone away completely. Physical tension and feelings of nervousness are troubling you less and less often, less and less severely all the time now. You find yourself more calm and relaxed. And because you are more calm and relaxed, stress, tension and anxiety are troubling you less and less often, less and less severely all the time now.

In addition, and as you feel necessary, include suggestions

i. to reduce feelings of depression (see p. 94)
ii. to lessen feelings of inferiority or increase your self-confidence (see Chapter 11)
iii. to use the five deep breaths as a 'trigger' for relaxation during moments of stress (see p. 65)
iv. for any other personal problems you find troublesome

We strongly recommend that you incorporate suggestions for using the five deep breaths as a trigger to relax in moments of tension or increased anxiety. Full instructions can be found on pages 65 and 67.

II: CONTROLLING ANXIETY IN SPECIFIC SITUATIONS

As you may have discovered from your own experience, anxiety can develop almost anywhere and at any time. Therefore we need hardly emphasise the usefulness of being able to control your own level of anxiety whenever necessary. For example, you may be very nervous in social situations. Or perhaps examinations or public speaking are an ordeal for you. Or you may be one of those people who experience anxiety in quite ordinary situations like waiting in a queue or being served in a restaurant. If you are a very sensitive sort of person, you may experience feelings of anxiety in crowded places or when you are out of doors. And men and women with a phobia will not need us to tell them that their anxiety can sometimes be so intense that it causes mental confusion and blind panic. In addition, the techniques described below will work even if you suddenly feel anxious but you don't know *why*. This last point is an interesting one, and we shall consider it at greater length.

Quite often, people who claim that they do not know why they feel anxious are able, with a little effort, to identify particular thoughts which occur immediately before feelings of alarm and anxiety.

For example, Philip, a newly-married 30–year-old freelance designer sought help because he began to experience attacks of anxiety when he was sitting at his desk working on the designs by which he earned his living. He reported that these anxiety attacks 'appeared from nowhere' while he was doing routine work on his designs. Each one started as a slightly nervous feeling which gradually developed as he tried to ignore it until it had become quite intense. Not unnaturally, he was rather disturbed by the whole problem and sought advice because he could not tolerate the disruption it caused.

Close questioning revealed a background of fairly high anxiety. Philip had given up his secure employment two years previously and had taken the gamble of self-employment. He had actually been very successful, but he had not planned his future very thoroughly, and as the work mounted up, he felt obliged to increase his working hours and work against increasingly tight deadlines to avoid disappointing his new clients. At the back of his mind, however, he had doubts about the wisdom of his decision in terms of future security and his relationship with his wife. The anxiety attacks seemed to develop when his mind turned over possible future problems while he was working. That process was almost subconscious; at least, he was not fully aware of the thoughts going through his mind. Some reassurance and a realistic appraisal of his abilities quickly convinced him that he had made the right choice, and the anxiety attacks died away.

Similarly, your anxiety should lessen of its own accord if you too can identify and come to terms with stressful thoughts in that way. However, that is not the main theme of this section, where we are chiefly concerned with the problem of coping with anxiety attacks, rather than explaining why they occur.

Anxiety 'feeds' on itself. An anxious person may notice his increasing tension, nervousness and mental confusion and think: 'Why do I feel this way? What's happening?' Such worried thoughts may produce further anxiety which in turn can make the physical and mental symptoms worse. The person then thinks: 'There's no reason to feel like this! I'm losing control!' The cycle of anxiety-tension-worry-anxiety is spiralling upwards, and it is at this stage that an anxious person may make an 'escape' from his anxiety-making situation – no matter what the cost. (The intense feelings of relief which are produced when the anxiety dissipates make almost any price seem worth paying!)

Fortunately, there are ways of controlling this anxiety. The first one is the 'emergency' five deep breaths method which we introduced as part of the self-hypnosis techniques explained in Chapter 4. However, taking a few deep breaths often controls anxiety, at least to a certain extent, whether or not you have tried those other techniques. This is because the procedure does two things. Firstly, it distracts you from your feelings of anxiety by transferring your attention on to a completely different matter, and secondly, it relaxes your body and releases tension. But of course it will be more effective if you *have* used the technique described in Chapter 4, because your subconscious mind will then already associate the five deep breaths with mental and physical relaxation. Therefore, if you haven't yet tried these techniques, you may like to do so now. The full method is described on pages 59–66.

This is how you can use the five deep breaths in moments of stress, alarm, arousal or anxiety during the day:

- STOP what you are doing
- Consciously RELAX your body as much as possible
- BREATHE IN slowly and deeply while mentally thinking or saying out loud: 'This tension is all . . .'
- BREATHE OUT while mentally thinking or saying aloud: '. . . going away.' Let yourself RELAX as you breathe out and feel the tension going away
- REPEAT that four times
- On the FIFTH cycle of inhalation/exhalation, substitute the words: 'This tension has all gone away completely'
- Use the procedure whenever you feel tension or anxiety beginning to develop

We cannot emphasise sufficiently that the more you practise this technique, the more effective it will become.

HOW TO CONTROL YOUR ANXIETY

As we have already explained, anxiety can spiral rapidly. This tends to happen if you do not notice the initial surge of adrenalin which occurs as a natural response to worried thoughts and stressful events. By the time you realise that you are becoming tense, it often seems impossible to do anything constructive to reduce the anxiety! The five deep breaths technique helps, but you may wish to avoid this particular aspect of the anxiety problem altogether by conditioning yourself to respond to shocks and startle (either physical or mental) *with relaxation instead of greater arousal.*

You can do this in the following way. First of all, record a series of loudish noises on a tape. Here are some examples: the sound of a doorbell, a dog barking, a metal plate crashing to the floor, two wooden blocks being banged together, the sound of someone clapping his or her hands. Record these noises at one-minute intervals on the tape. Then sit or lie down with the tape recorder nearby. Shut your eyes and relax completely: this should not be difficult if you have used the self-hypnosis or relaxation techniques. Next, start the tape. At intervals, you will hear a fairly loud and unexpected noise, to which your body will react with the normal 'startle response' – a surge of adrenalin and increased arousal. (This is usually most noticeable as a sinking feeling in the pit of your stomach.) After each noise, you must consciously bring your body and mind back to a state of relaxation. The next noise on the tape will of course increase your arousal once again. So you must relax once more. In other words, each time a noise startles you, bring your body back to a state of complete relaxation. You may need more time to do this at first – if so, stop the tape. It is essential to be relaxed; otherwise, you might condition yourself to respond to shocks and startle with even greater arousal than you do at the moment!

Initially, you may not be able to detect much difference in your body's response to these sudden stimuli, but if you practise this exercise over a period of several days, sooner or later you will find that your body accepts the noise as a signal to relax. When you have achieved this, you can establish the same reaction to worried thoughts. Simply relax, and think of something which makes you uneasy. As before, notice the surge of adrenalin – and then consciously relax once again. Repeat this as often as necessary over a period of several days until your body responds to worrying and startling thoughts with relaxation and *not* greater arousal. As you can probably see, these two techniques are very effective methods of helping yourself to remain calm and relaxed in your everyday routine.

Sometimes the effects of anxiety are so severe that it *seems* uncontrollable. In reality, this is never the case, because anxiety can always be alleviated – if you know how. One very important point is this: anxiety, despite all its unpleasant mental and physical effects, is actually quite harmless. Perhaps you fear anxiety because you believe that it 'will do some damage'. That is absolute nonsense – although you may find the assertion hard to believe when you feel panic-stricken and you are immobilised in terror with your heart palpitating and your breathing upset! The techniques described below will help you to 'ride through' an anxiety attack without running away, panicking, or developing a greater fear of anxiety in the future. (These following ideas are based on the research work of Dr Claire Weekes.)

1. *Face* your anxiety and acknowledge that it is happening. Do not try to ignore or avoid it by using a coping or defence mechanism (these are explained in Chapter 1) such as throwing yourself into another activity or even simply 'running away from it'.
2. *Accept* your physical and emotional feelings without self-criticism, self-condemnation or efforts to fight the anxiety. Remember that tensing the body muscles or thinking worried thoughts such as 'Oh God, I can't cope!' will actually increase your anxiety.

    However, in suggesting you should 'accept your feelings', we do not mean that you should concentrate on them. Rather, simply acknowledge those feelings and then turn your attention to something else. One anxious person told us that he sometimes feels the muscles in his legs begin to tremble when he is under stress. He then thinks, 'There it is again! Oh well, never mind, it will soon go away', and turns his attention to whatever he is doing. This, he said, not only prevents his anxiety from growing, but also stops him worrying about it. (We discuss how one's thoughts and attention can affect the extent of one's anxiety in Chapter 10.)

3. *Relax* your body. It may seem impossible to relax in the face of severe anxiety amounting perhaps to panic, but it can be done. Claire Weekes (1977) has written that one can 'float' past a 'whipping flash of panic' by 'taking the panic with as little resistance as possible; by waiting until the flash spends itself and then going on with the job on hand'.

    You can help yourself to relax by doing it willingly, not as though it is some unavoidable, unpleasant task. You should: STOP what you are doing; consciously relax any tense parts of your body such as your shoulders, your facial muscles, your hands, and so on; breathe slowly and deeply using the five deep breaths technique as described earlier; and allow tension to dissipate each time you breathe out.

4. Do not *worry about time*. That is, time in any sense: the duration of an anxiety attack, an imagined need to be 'doing something else', the frequency of your anxiety attacks, or whatever. Most anxious people hope to get through difficult situations by rushing blindly at them, but such an approach only increases the likelihood that you will feel anxious. If you take life slowly and calmly, you will have much more control over the events that happen to you. So slow down, look around you, and take note of your surroundings. You may be surprised by the amount of interesting detail which you normally miss. The point is, of course, that by behaving in such a way, you help to cultivate a generally more relaxed state of mind and body.

OTHER EFFECTS OF ANXIETY

In this section, we shall briefly discuss a few of the more extreme effects which anxiety can have on the human body. These effects can be very alarming; indeed, many people who experience them rush to a doctor with the firm conviction that they are physically ill. We therefore hope that this section will provide both reassurance and explanation. The problems which we discuss are:

- depersonalisation and derealisation
- panic and palpitations (irregular heartbeats)
- 'difficulty in breathing or swallowing'
- feelings of collapse, muscular weakness or 'trembling'

Depersonalisation and derealisation

Depersonalisation and derealisation are two variations of the same experience. *Depersonalisation* refers to a feeling of separation from your body; *derealisation* to a feeling of separation from your surroundings. During depersonalisation, an individual feels as though he has become removed, cut off or disembodied from himself. He feels as though he is a detached observer looking down from a separate place, dispassionately watching himself and his actions. The feeling lasts anything from a few seconds to a few hours and starts and stops abruptly. Derealisation may involve mild feelings of unreality which persist for weeks; this is even more bizarre because it seems as though you are separate from the world in which you are walking about! Perhaps the nearest analogy is a theatrical one – you are in the environment of the production, but not a part of the production itself. Both these types of feelings of unreality are a natural consequence of 'too much anxious introspection', which of course means that one tends to concentrate on one's own feelings and experiences rather than on what is happening in the world around one.

The best way of dealing with depersonalisation and derealisation is simply to accept the feelings as a natural part of anxiety, because the problem eases when one stops worrying about the way one feels. It becomes even less troublesome as any background anxiety also decreases.

Panic and palpitations (strong or irregular heartbeats)

The key to understanding feelings of panic lies in the fact that anxiety tends to escalate. This is because panic is not so much caused by a fear of a place or situation or object, as by a fear of the mental and physical symptoms of anxiety. An anxious person may respond to small shocks or startle with exaggerated arousal ('first fear'). The anxious individual then notices his pounding heart, increasing tension and feelings of apprehension, whereupon he or she begins to worry about what will happen next ('second fear'). And, as we have already explained, such thoughts produce even more anxiety and tension – until it spirals out of control, accompanied by a frighteningly strong belief that 'something terrible' is about to happen.

Palpitations are alarming and may even make a person wonder if his heart is about to stop or even burst. This may sound slightly amusing, but it represents a real fear for some people. Of course, the heart will neither stop nor burst, however strong or irregular its beats may be.

Both panic and palpitations become less noticeable as anxiety decreases. However, if you find that they are especially troublesome, you can tackle them with self-hypnosis. For the tape recorder technique, suitable suggestions would include: 'Panic and palpitations are troubling you less and less often, less and less severely all the time now.'

Difficulty in breathing or swallowing

Anxiety can increase tension in the muscles of the throat and chest to the point where it may seem impossible to swallow or to expand the chest. However, the brain will not allow breathing to stop for so long that any harm occurs, and it is only muscle tension produced by anxiety which prevents a normal breathing rhythm from being maintained. Thus, if your breathing becomes irregular during an anxiety attack, you should not worry about it, for that will only make the tension worse. Simply make a relaxed conscious effort to bring it back to normal. Do not, however, breathe too rapidly or too deeply for too long, because that will remove too much carbon dioxide from the blood and may lead to dizziness or cause a tingling sensation in the muscles. If this happens, you may find that your subconscious breathing control centre temporarily stops your breathing while a normal balance is restored.

Difficulty in swallowing or a 'lump in the throat' are also extremely common effects of anxiety. They are, once again, a result of muscle tension. Although uncomfortable, they certainly do not usually indicate any serious problem (but see 'other effects' below).

Feelings of collapse, muscular 'weakness' or trembling

These feelings are caused by the interaction of sympathetic and parasympathetic nervous systems, which influence opposing muscles in the skeletal system. Additionally, diversion of blood to and from the skin can cause slight feelings of dizziness or giddiness as one's blood pressure fluctuates. Although these effects may be very marked, they do not signify any real muscular weakness, and the way to overcome them is to accept them, avoid worrying about them, relax and direct your attention to the task in hand.

Other effects

The stress associated with anxiety can produce many other symptoms: pain, visual disturbances, peculiar mental sensations, apparently real physical 'illness' and so on. It is important to understand that such symptoms can be expected with anxiety, and are not a sign of physical illness. Nevertheless, it is clearly sensible to see a doctor to obtain confirmation of that fact before dealing with your anxiety.

COPING WITH THE PHYSICAL (AND MENTAL) EFFECTS OF ANXIETY

Occasionally, the physical effects of anxiety can be really inconvenient and embarrassing. For example, a businessman anxious about meeting people may find that his palms are damp with perspiration, and this can make personal introductions and shaking hands into an ordeal. (If you shake hands with someone whose palms are sweating, you know he is anxious – and it simply isn't very pleasant, anyway.) In cases like these, self-hypnosis can be helpful. We have already indicated how you could use specific suggestions to deal with feelings of panic and palpitations. Another example, for the businessman mentioned above, might be: 'You are becoming more calm and relaxed when you are meeting people. You find that hand perspiration and feelings of nervousness are troubling you less and less all the time now.'

This kind of treatment should produce a gradual and steady improvement. In combination with the other techniques described in this chapter, it represents a powerful tool for self-change, and you should either take it seriously or leave it alone.

REFERENCE

Weekes, C. (1977). *Agoraphobia: Simple, Effective Treatment*, p. 32. Angus and Robertson, London.

9. Fears and Phobias

A phobia can be defined as an intense anxiety reaction, in which specific stimuli that arouse the reaction can be identified, and in which the feared object actually lacks the dangerous qualities expected by the individual concerned. What this means, simply, is that the intensity of a phobic individual's reaction to the object of his phobia is out of all proportion to the actual danger. In this chapter, we shall explain how a person can come to fear an object, event or situation which is, in reality, quite harmless. We shall also examine the problems which phobias can cause.

HOW PHOBIAS DEVELOP

I: CONDITIONING

In Chapter 7, we explained that if you experience anxiety in a particular situation, you may later feel anxiety in other similar situations. This *conditioned* anxiety – or 'fear' – is often strong and tends to recur many times in the future. The process is beautifully illustrated by a Dutch girl with claustrophobia. She remembered being shut into a coal-bunker by a woman who was supposed to be looking after her while her mother was ill. She described the experience in this way: 'I was shut in . . . pitch black everywhere and choking in coal dust, forgotten all day. I still shiver when I think about it. For years I could not be left alone and had nightmares galore' (Melville, 1977). Obviously this brutal punishment had terrified her, and the psychological pain and trauma which it had produced were evoked by any remotely similar situations later in life.

The mechanism of conditioning ensures that we can develop a

phobia about literally anything. However, some phobias (for example, the fear of spiders, snakes and high places) are unquestionably more common than others, an observation which has led Dr Seligman of Pennsylvania University to suggest that humans are predisposed to develop certain fears. It is indeed true that the most common phobic objects such as snakes or insects might have represented one of the more dangerous environmental influences during the evolution of our ancestors. Although this idea is mostly speculation, it is supported to some extent by the observation that babies avoid the edges of surfaces above the ground – as though they are instinctively afraid of heights.

In contrast, we know for sure that a person's level of arousal during a traumatic event (or series of events) is a factor of great importance in determining whether or not he or she develops a phobia as a result of that event. As you may recall, this is because conditioning is much more effective if one is highly aroused. Now, the extent to which one becomes aroused in any situation depends in part upon how one perceives that situation. Consider, for example, a fear of the dark. As a child, you may have vividly imagined all sorts of dangers lurking in the dark. If your parents did not discourage these childish fears, you might have been frightened very easily by strange or unexpected noises at night. Clearly, the more anxious you became, the greater the likelihood that you would develop a fear of the dark.

Many phobias develop during childhood because at that stage of our lives we may not have the mental and physical ability to cope with stressful experiences in a rational way. The next two cases illustrate this point. The first concerns a middle-aged woman who had a phobia about dogs which was so severe that she became physically ill if one so much as touched her. Investigation revealed that when she was a very young child, a dog had jumped up at her, knocked her over, and dragged her along the road by pulling her coat. Although as an adult the woman knew that dogs are usually quite harmless, her subconscious mind had been conditioned by the experience and so she continued to feel fear whenever she saw a dog. (Incidentally, this emphasises the protective function of the conditioning process – that is, to keep us away from whatever has been a source of danger in the past.)

The second case concerns a woman with a phobic fear of cats. This lady clearly remembered the incident which had started the problem: at the age of four, her father had drowned a favourite kitten in front of her. When, at the age of 14, her parents placed a fur coat inside her bed, she became hysterical; and when she was 18, the sight of a cat produced another bout of hysteria. After this, her phobia continued to develop, until, by the time she was 30, her fear of cats was so marked that she refused to walk out of doors on her own. Nor would she enter a room or house where she suspected there might be a cat. Even touching her daughter's furry teddy bear upset her! There are two especially interesting points about this case. Firstly, the woman did not feel anxious when she *actually saw* a cat – rather, she spent much of her time in a state of fear that she *might* see one. This kind of irrational fear may be the 'final straw' which actually impels a phobic person to seek help. Secondly, the woman's fear had *generalised* from the original stimulus – a cat – to other vaguely similar objects, including the teddy bear (Eysenck, 1977).

This process of generalisation is frequently observed with phobic anxiety. For example, Helen is a friend of ours who has had a fear of heights since she was 15. Her phobia developed when she was lying on a cliff-top with some schoolfriends. One of the boys grabbed her arm and pretended that he was going to push her over. Helen was extremely frightened and alarmed, even though the boy quickly released her. Ever since then, she has felt dizzy each time she's been near a cliff-edge, and she has avoided high places as much as possible. Interestingly she is also scared of flying although she manages to travel on planes, albeit with mild discomfort and anxiety. It seems likely that this is a generalisation of her fear of heights, rather than a genuine fear of flying.

In the examples described above, the individuals involved knew how their phobias had developed, but this is not always the case: some phobias originate in long-forgotten childhood experiences; others, as we shall see, result from more complicated causes.

Before we move on, let us emphasise once again that the way in which we view any potentially stressful event determines the effect which it will have on us. Consider, for example, the fears of snakes and spiders. Our reaction to these animals is frequently much more dramatic than can be justified by reason of any danger involved. If someone comes across a spider or snake and subsequently develops a phobia, we may assume that he or she believes these animals to be more dangerous than they actually are.

'Social phobias'

As we mentioned earlier, it is possible to develop a phobia about any object, situation or event. Thus, for example, many people find that the idea of eating in public causes them intense anxiety. Other people have a morbid fear of seeing anyone else vomiting, or indeed of vomiting themselves. And for many men and women, public speaking is a major ordeal. So-called 'social phobias' like these develop in much the same way as the more well-known phobias about insects, flying, high places, and such like.

To illustrate this, let us consider a young man who has had too much to drink at a party. He begins to feel nauseous and heads for the toilet, but he vomits before he can get there. He then feels very embarrassed and extremely anxious. He worries about what the other guests will think of him; he may feel deeply ashamed. Next time he goes out, he becomes extremely anxious about the possibility of being sick or seeing someone else being sick. The slightest murmur from his stomach increases his anxiety. He may even make himself so anxious that he actually is sick. In any event, if his anxiety is intense, he will probably begin to avoid social occasions in the future.

We mentioned earlier that a common phobia centres on anxiety about eating in public. Quite often this phobia develops after an embarrassing or alarming experience such as having a fish-bone stick in your throat or coughing violently after you've swallowed a drink 'the wrong way'. Although a person who experiences an unfortunate incident like this will probably feel better very quickly, he may be surprised to find that next time he sits down to eat a meal, he feels more and more anxious. As so often, this anxiety gradually increases – perhaps to the point where it is impossible to eat or drink in public.

Intense anxiety about situations which involve other people may arise in a slightly different way. Suppose, for example, that a person's quite normal anxiety in a particular situation results in a slight stammer, a blush to the face, a slight shaking of the hands or a need to visit the toilet. Such reactions are, of course, quite normal (for example, even the most accomplished public speakers sometimes find that their hands are shaking, even if they do not feel nervous). Unfortunately, they can also be very embarrassing. And as one's embarrassment begins to mount, with thoughts such as 'Oh no, what will all these people think of me?' one's anxiety also increases. This in itself makes the problem worse. But as if that wasn't bad enough, as soon as you focus your attention on a muscular tremble, a blush to your cheeks, a need to visit the loo or a slight stammer, they all begin to seem more obvious and more urgent!

Now, some people can laugh off such experiences and never worry about them again. But other people are acutely sensitive to this kind of embarrassment and worry, and next time they are in a similar situation, they will experience considerable anxiety about the possibility of the same thing happening again. Worry like this is the first step in what could become a self-fulfilling prophecy: in other words, you worry about blushing, stammering, trembling, saying the wrong thing, or one of a hundred other problems, and before you know it, your anxiety is so intense that it has actually happened! You then feel an overwhelming urge to escape from the anxiety-producing situation – and never to return in the future!

We may include other common fears and worries within this poorly defined category of 'social phobia'. For example, there are many anxious people who believe – quite wrongly – that 'everyone is looking at me'. Such worries centre on a fear of being the focus of attention. An individual with this type of anxiety problem may become so self-conscious that he will not enter a room of strangers or walk past other men and women at, say, a bus-stop. Sometimes anxiety centres on worries that one's body is unusual, ridiculous or amusing. Again, this can develop into an extreme self-consciousness; this time, about revealing one's body in a swimming costume, and such like.

It is not so easy to explain the origin of fears like these. The cause is probably a complicated mixture of: a poor self-image; unpleasant past experiences in childhood and adolescence (a time at which one's developing sense of self-identity and self-esteem is very vulnerable to the ridicule of one's peers);

conditioned anxiety from unpleasant experiences in adulthood; and other repressed fears and worries.

But perhaps the most common 'social phobia' of all is intense anxiety when meeting other people – or at the thought of meeting other people. Of course, nearly all of us experience at least some initial anxiety in social situations. Shy people, however, often experience such intense anxiety that they really can be said to have 'a fear of meeting people'. Sometimes it is hard to distinguish between 'normal' anxiety, self-consciousness and shyness, and this more extreme form. We shall therefore discuss the topic as a whole in Chapter 11.

II: REPRESSION

In Chapter 1, we explained how thoughts, feelings and emotions which a person finds unacceptable may be repressed from the conscious to the subconscious mind. In Chapter 8, we mentioned that repression can cause persistent anxiety; in this chapter, we shall explain how repression can be responsible for the development of phobic anxiety. The process starts when a consciously unacceptable fear or worry is repressed into the subconscious mind, which then appears to 'search' for something symbolic on to which the original feelings of fear and anxiety can be projected. As a result, the apparent object of the phobia actually masks the real fear. Some examples will help to illustrate this idea.

Dr Paul Hauck (1981) described a case of a phobia which he believes had its origin in repressed feelings of guilt and worry. It concerns a young woman with an irrational fear of snakes and lizards. This bothered her to such an extent that every night when she went to bed she felt compelled to check all the bedding. Her fear also generalised on to insects, so that if she saw a centipede or worm on the ground, she would take refuge in her house in panic. When she began to talk of moving house so as to avoid these animals, she was persuaded to obtain professional help. After some discussion with her doctor, the cause of the problem emerged: as a child, she had been sexually assaulted by her cousin. However, she had not told her parents because she thought they might blame her for the incident. Rather, she repressed all her memories of the event, presumably with the feelings of guilt and anxiety which it had produced. After her marriage, her sexual activity reawakened memories of that childhood experience and the guilt and shame she had felt. All the distressing emotions and feelings which she recalled became associated with sexual activity and were transferred in symbolic form on to these small animals. Interestingly, when she began to discuss the childhood experience, her shame and guilt vanished and her phobia went with it. This does not always happen.

On a more general level, the repression of specific worries about life, work, sex and social matters can cause a phobia to develop. For example, a man may repress some social or sexual problem into his subconscious, which then 'projects' the original fear on to something quite different. Thus, the reasoning implies, a man might repress his worries about social failure or feelings of inferiority – but then develop a fear of lifts. This *fear of lifts* is in fact a *fear of falling down the lift shaft*, which in turn really represents a *fear of 'falling' socially*. As another example, consider a person who fears success (or the responsibility attached to success). This fear could become a fear of heights. Other products of this repression and projection process could include a fear of ladders, looking over the tops of buildings and so on. Incidentally, people often experience strong thoughts or fears when they are on top of high cliffs or buildings. These frequently take the form of an irrational worry that you might throw yourself over the edge. Similarly, you may have experienced an irrational urge to drive your car at a brick wall. Presumably feelings and thoughts like these consciously represent a subconscious fear of 'not being in control of oneself'.

The logical development of these ideas is that a phobia sometimes acts as a defence mechanism which helps a person to avoid the real cause of his anxiety. Consider these statements:

- If only I wasn't afraid of flying, *I could take that job in America*.
- If only I didn't have a phobia about her dogs, *I could move in and live with my girlfriend*.
- I feel so awful when I'm in an enclosed room. *It stops me joining my friends and colleagues at parties and restaurants*.

In each case, the person concerned might be using his phobia to avoid doing something which would cause him even more anxiety. Thus, if *you* have a phobia, try asking yourself what you would do if the phobia was suddenly removed. Your answer may reveal the real cause of your fear.

You may at this point be wondering whether it is possible to treat a phobia without a full knowledge and understanding of how and why it originally developed. This is actually a somewhat difficult and controversial topic. Freudian psychologists in particular have maintained that treatment of a phobia is only possible if the full psychological background is known. Behavioural psychologists, on the other hand, have claimed a 90 per cent success rate for the treatment of phobias – without any reference to the original cause of the problem. We may therefore assume that one can safely treat a phobia without probing into its origins, so long as any associated anxiety, depression and personality problems are dealt with at the same time.

Worry and Phobias

Usually a phobic person only experiences anxiety when he or she comes into contact with the object of his or her phobia. But as we have already seen, phobic anxiety sometimes develops into a constant, more-or-less intense anxiety centred on the possibility of actually coming across the phobic object. Watts (1973) described the case of a hospital porter who seems to have had an anxiety problem of this sort. The man in question was obsessed by thoughts about the Russians. He was always making strange remarks about them, and whenever a plane flew over, he dived under a table – presumably because he feared a Russian invasion.

This kind of irrational fear or worry is probably rather more common than you might imagine. It can take many different forms; in every case, though, the person concerned cannot perceive or accept that his fear is irrational (even if there is a fragment of reality at the bottom of the problem). In passing, we should perhaps speculate on the role which newspapers and TV play in promoting needless fear and anxiety.

The intense and persistent but totally irrational nature of fears such as these strongly suggests that repression and projection have taken place. In other words, that a person has repressed some worry or other emotional problem into his or her subconscious, and that his subconscious has then projected the emotional problem on to the feared object or event. If this is so, it might be important to identify and deal with the underlying problem when the obvious phobia is treated.

ILLNESS PHOBIAS

Many people have a morbid fear of illness or death. These phobias may be a straightforward anxiety problem like the fears of spiders, enclosed spaces and cats described at the start of this chapter. On the other hand, they may become associated with intense irrational worry.

Perhaps not surprisingly, many illness phobias centre on the most well-known (and feared) diseases in our society: in particular, heart disease and cancer. One woman whom we shall call Jill (not her real name) was tormented by her fear of cancer for several years. This phobia apparently started after a period of personal stress which left her feeling anxious and depressed. She then came across an account of a cancer victim in a magazine and immediately grasped the idea that her own discomfort was caused by the same illness.

She began to imagine that any bruise on her skin would develop into a cancerous growth; she had also read that body moles and freckles could enlarge and become cancerous, so she kept going to her doctor for check-ups. Eventually, much of her time was spent looking for any abnormal signs of the illness, and even imagining that other people were discussing it. Any reference to cancer caused her acute anxiety, for in some vague way she believed she was likely to develop it. A thorough medical examination which revealed no signs of the disease convinced her she was not physically ill and she experienced a great sense of relief. Unfortunately, however, this relief was short-lived and the problem soon returned. The intensity of her anxiety varied according to the stress she experienced in her personal life, and it seemed clear that the cancer phobia masked some deeper worry, although it was not clear what this was. Eventually the problem cleared up of its own accord, presumably as Jill came to terms with her underlying problems.

We should emphasise that not all worries about health or

physical appearance are neurotic forms of anxiety; far from it. In fact, many people suffer great agonies of mind because they genuinely believe that some aspect of their health, appearance or behaviour is 'abnormal'. Worries like these may seem to be reasonable but they are usually based on a lack of information or knowledge. An example may be that a person suddenly notices the presence of taste buds at the back of the tongue and thinks this to be some sort of abnormal growth until reassured by a doctor.

Inevitably, perhaps, many such worries are sexual. In a society where we are constantly bombarded with so much propaganda about our behaviour and our bodies, is it any wonder that people may begin to worry about whether or not they match up to a 'desirable standard'? What may be cause for greater concern is the fact that so many adolescents (and adults) suffer needless anxiety about sex, when simple information would reassure them. Some books which may be helpful and reassuring for people with sexual and other worries are listed in Further Reading, page 163.

However, to return to the main theme of this section: why should someone develop a phobia about illness? (Remember that phobia means '*irrational* fear'.) There are probably many, many reasons. Let us consider a few possible ones. To start with, the emotional trauma of watching a friend or relative with a serious illness may produce considerable emotional stress. Not surprisingly, perhaps, this can take the form of intense worry that one has the same illness. Secondly, a person may repress some other fear or worry and subsequently develop an illness phobia. For example, a phobia about infection with sexual disease could be caused by worries about sexual activity of a sort which made you feel guilty. Thirdly, the shock of one's own illness might produce anxiety and thereby predispose one to develop a phobia. Fourthly, we may suppose that a child brought up by parents who were excessively concerned with health (or illness) is likely to associate his emotional problems with his health. No doubt there are also other reasons. But quite frequently, there is a background of general personality problems such as a lack of confidence or a low self-esteem: and it is not difficult to see how an illness phobia or intense worry might really represent a subconscious call for help, attention or sympathy on the part of an anxious or depressed or otherwise emotionally distressed individual.

Many people with illness phobias constantly ask for reassurance from the people around them. Even if this is forthcoming, it usually has only a transient effect, and the sufferer soon begins asking for reassurance again. But because reassurance does temporarily reduce anxiety, it is difficult to stop asking 'I'm not ill, am I?' Those around a person with an illness phobia – or any other irrational worry – should realise the importance of withholding reassurance, even in the face of intense and persistent questioning.

AGORAPHOBIA

Agoraphobia has been called a 'social disease' of our highly stressed, present-day world. It accounts for about 75 per cent of all the phobias, and 90 per cent of the sufferers are women, yet it is little understood among the general public.

Agoraphobia is usually thought of as 'a fear of open spaces'. Yet this is not exactly true; a sufferer seems to fear shops, crowded places, confined places, travelling away from home, situations where other people are in close proximity, and so on. In fact what really underlies this problem is that all agoraphobics fear *an attack of anxiety* if they move away from home. A person with agoraphobia prefers to stay at home rather than risk an anxiety attack in a public place because the anxiety attacks associated with agoraphobia can be extremely alarming. Indeed, the sufferer may even think she is dying. This is especially true if she feels palpitations, a raised heart beat, and has difficulty in breathing or swallowing.

So how does this unusual and distressing condition develop? Most often, agoraphobia is nothing more than another form of conditioned emotional response. A typical sequence of events in its development might be something like this: a person who is under some degree of stress has a mild attack of palpitations, a fainting episode, feelings of dizziness, or some similar experience one day when he or she is out of the house. Now, many people would be able to dismiss such an episode as insignificant. Others, however, would become embarrassed or anxious. They might, for example, dread 'losing control' or 'making a scene' in front of other people. A woman like this would probably feel that she must avoid public exposure by leaving the place where the attack occurred as soon as possible. But this may not be easy if there are other people about. She becomes more worried and tense, both mentally and physically. As this tension begins to increase, a vicious circle develops: greater anxiety produces more tension which then produces more anxiety. The palpitations, dizziness and so on then become even worse.

Eventually the woman manages to get home. She feels 'safe' and her anxiety dies away. However, the damage has been done – fear of the same thing happening again now dominates her life and she may prefer to stay at home rather than risk another anxiety attack. If she does venture outside, the mechanism of the subconscious conditioned response is easily evoked: an attack of anxiety can be generated merely by memory of her previous experience. This keeps her away from anywhere likely to produce a similar reaction. Hence: home is 'safe', outside is 'dangerous'. Sometimes an agoraphobic screws up all her courage and ventures outside. This use of will-power produces an increase in tension – so much so that the muscles of her body may become 'locked' tight and literally root her to the spot. Relief is only obtained by turning and fleeing homewards – and then, of course, her desire to remain indoors is heightened.

Many agoraphobic people are generally highly aroused and anxious. This means that even trivial and insignificant events can be very alarming and have a major effect in setting off an outbreak of panic. Each person or object becomes a major obstacle to movement. Is it surprising that under such emotional strain, an agoraphobic finds it easier to stay at home?

Frequently, this particular aspect of the problem is compounded by the so-called 'concerned husband syndrome'. He takes over the shopping, delivering the children to school, and other duties, thereby leaving his wife trapped with no motivation to go out, and her self-confidence and self-respect gradually disappear altogether.

Sometimes this drawing-in of horizons follows a slightly different course. Claire Weekes has described how an agoraphobic may begin to avoid fast trains because she can't get off quickly if she experiences an anxiety attack. Unfortunately, slow trains soon become a site of panic attacks, and so she turns to buses. When panic attacks develop on buses, she restricts herself to walking. This clearly limits her range, but even so, she may still feel anxious. Before long, she walks no further than the end of the road, and eventually she 'cannot' leave the house at all.

Presumably agoraphobia can also represent a psychological defence mechanism against circumstances which an individual finds unacceptable. In one case, a university student became progressively more anxious as he tried to travel from his home to college. Investigation revealed that his parents had pressured him into university against his wishes. He also found the academic standards rather high. Perhaps rather than directly counter his parents' wishes, he developed the oblique resistance of agoraphobia as an expression of his desire to start a career directly after leaving school.

There are probably many other types of situation in which agoraphobia acts as a psychological defence mechanism. Suppose a husband is made redundant, and his family experiences a dramatic change in its financial fortunes. If his wife is an oversensitive person, and the stress is too much to bear, she may develop agoraphobia. Partly this represents a fear of meeting people because of the shame she feels about her newly impoverished financial situation; partly also it represents a desperate clinging to her home as a symbol of the material success into which she has invested so much effort over the years. In effect, she believes she is protecting her family's home and reputation.

Whatever the cause of agoraphobia, if the individual concerned lives in a suburban area where people 'keep themselves to themselves', his or her isolation may rapidly increase.

Yet another cause of agoraphobia is a form of depressive illness. The agoraphobic conditions described above are usually approached by means of relaxation and other behavioural treatment. We shall now describe how this can be done.

SELF-HELP TREATMENT FOR PHOBIAS

One treatment which has produced many successful results in recent years is *desensitisation*. This works for all phobias if you approach the method with determination (and remember that any associated anxiety, depression, phobias, worries or personality problems should also be treated at the same time).

The basis of desensitisation is deep relaxation. To illustrate how this can overcome a phobia, let us consider a hypothetical case of a man who wishes to overcome his phobia about dogs. David, as we shall call him, starts by learning how to relax completely (see Chapter 3). He must then spend some time giving careful consideration to the extent of his phobia. Obviously, if the very thought of a dog produces anxiety, it will be necessary for him to do this while he is completely relaxed. Each time any tension begins to develop, he will stop and relax again before he continues his analysis.

First of all, David considers whether he has one or more basic fears about dogs; for example, does he fear that the dog may be carrying fleas or disease, or is the phobia simply related to a fear of being bitten? A related point would be the extent of any generalisation or 'spreading' of his fears.

David's next step is to establish a list of situations which provoke his anxiety. For example, he realises that a picture of a dog produces much less anxiety than the sound of a dog barking, and that small dogs produce less anxiety than large ones. Careful thought, while he is relaxed, allows him to establish a list or *hierarchy* of anxiety-producing situations:

1. looking at a picture of puppies
2. touching the same picture
3. looking at a picture of a small dog
4. listening to dogs barking late at night
5. watching dogs on television
6. looking at puppies in a pet shop
7. touching a child's stuffed toy dog
8. walking along a street and seeing a dog some distance away
9. walking past a fully-grown dog on the other side of the road
10. being touched unexpectedly by a fully-grown dog
11. touching or stroking a puppy
12. touching a medium-sized dog
13. touching a fully-grown large dog such as an alsatian

Compiling such a list is the basis of all desensitisation treatment of phobia, and you should therefore take the time and trouble to do it thoroughly. If thinking about the object of your phobia makes you feel anxious, stop and relax. Also, be careful to identify your basic fears correctly. For example, if you find that you have more than one basic fear, you will need to establish two (or more) hierarchies. You can deal with the less disturbing one first. You may find it helpful to set a target date by which you are determined to be able to carry out a particular objective, for example, eating fish, stroking a dog, going to the dentist, receiving an injection or looking down from a high building.

After you have made these preparations, you are ready to move on to the desensitisation treatment itself. There are two ways of doing this: *in imagination* and *in vivo* (i.e. in 'life').

DESENSITISATION IN IMAGINATION

To use this technique, you relax completely and visualise yourself successively in each of the anxiety-producing situations on your hierarchy, starting with the least anxiety-making and progressing upwards. The objective is to cultivate a detailed, complete and vivid image of each situation as though you were actually taking part in it – but to do this while your body and mind are as relaxed as possible. You should spend sufficient time on each level of the hierarchy to be sure that you can remain relaxed while you mentally visualise the scene: and, if any anxiety does develop, you should consciously relax your mind and body to relieve it. When you are satisfied with your achievement at each level, you can move on to the next one in the hierarchy.

If you can consistently relax at one level of the hierarchy, but not at the next, you are probably trying to take too large a step at one go. You can solve this problem by inserting another stage into your hierarchy.

Clearly, the longer you spend on the procedure, the more effective it will be. Sometimes you can achieve better results if you practise mental imagery before you start the desensitisation itself. You can do this by relaxing deeply, closing your eyes and imagining brightly coloured shapes and objects.

Desensitisation in imagination is very effective, but it may not remove *all* your phobic anxiety. You may feel satisfied if you reduce your anxiety to some degree (remember that there are techniques described in Chapter 8 which will help you to control any residual anxiety); on the other hand, you may wish to complete the process by moving on to desensitisation *in vivo*.

DESENSITISATION *in vivo*

This is essentially similar to the procedure above, in that you work through your hierarchy, achieving both mental and physical relaxation at each level before moving on to the next. This time, however, you are doing it for real. In other words, you will use real situations, events or objects connected with your phobia, perhaps together with models and photographs of it. (No matter how obscure or bizarre your phobia may be, with a little effort you can usually obtain suitable photographs or models; exactly what these are will depend on your hierarchy, of course.) Obviously, this method increases the chance that you will feel some anxiety. But the important point is that by progressing up a hierarchy in this way, you will be able to control the extent of that anxiety, and thereby avoid the need to escape from the phobic situation. One advantage of desensitisation *in vivo* is that by looking at or touching photographs, models and objects related to the phobia, you will obtain a real proof of your ability to remain calm and relaxed at each level of your hierarchy.

OTHER EXAMPLES OF DESENSITISATION

We have already described one hierarchy for the densensitisation of a phobia about dogs. Let us now briefly consider phobias which centre on a situation rather than an object. For example, you could treat a phobia about *lifts* by first visualising yourself inside one, travelling up and down, and then doing so in reality. You might watch people getting in and out of a lift from successively closer points, then touch the 'call' button, then get inside and travel one floor up or down, then two floors, and so on. You would of course ensure that you were relaxed at each stage of this progression before moving on to the next.

A fear of *the dark* might be treated in the following way. To start with, you would need to black out a room of your home. You would then position a lamp which you could switch on and off to one side of a comfortable chair. Next, you would sit down and relax. By switching off the light for progressively longer periods of time, you should be able to accustom yourself to the dark. Each time any anxiety began to develop, you would switch the light on and relax before sitting in the darkness again. (As an adjunct to this procedure, it is helpful to use your senses of touch, hearing and sight to increase your familiarity with the environment which has previously frightened you.) Clearly, at some point, you will want to extend your anxiety-control training to environments outside your home.

Overcoming agoraphobia

It is not enough to merely alleviate the symptoms of agoraphobia by coming to depend on someone else accompanying you whenever you go out. Nor is it enough to use 'props' such as travelling in a car whenever necessary, hiding behind dark glasses, or pushing a pram or shopping trolley, for these are only crutches which conceal the basic problem. However, no matter how serious your agoraphobia may seem to be, you should be able to make considerable improvement *if you approach the problem with enough motivation*.

To start with, consider the extent and basis of your anxiety. Is it a fear of 'losing control' in front of other people? Is it a fear of the effects of anxiety? Do you worry about what others will think? (One agoraphobic told us that she would feel 'stupid' if she fainted in public, yet she could not tell us why. Probably such thoughts result from the belief that 'losing control' is the same as 'not being in control of oneself', and the person concerned may well have a subconscious fear of this.) Ask yourself why you are so concerned with other people's opinions. Do they really matter? And, anyway, how can you be sure what other people will think or do? Remember that our own impressions about other people's attitudes and behaviour are often quite wrong. You may, for example, believe that other people will condemn or criticise you for 'losing control' or fainting, whereas in actual fact, most people feel only concern and a desire to help if they see someone else in trouble. If in fact you decide that concern for other people's standards and opinions rather than your own is a contributory factor to your agoraphobia, you should begin a process of self-examination and analysis to decide which of your beliefs and attitudes is causing you emotional distress.

Remember that we suggested agoraphobia can be a psychological defence against more subtle emotional problems. Thus, your willingness to spend time 'thinking through' your agoraphobia could be an indication of how much you 'need' to keep it. Once again, you may find it enlightening to ask yourself what would be the first thing you'd do if your agoraphobia was immediately taken away. Could that be what you really are afraid of? For example, meeting people, having to accept an unpleasant job, and so on. We are not suggesting that all cases of agoraphobia have a hidden cause like this – but some do.

Coming to terms with your own psychology can be a slow and lengthy business. Obviously, agoraphobics need other effective, short-term methods of self-help.

Since many people with phobias are emotionally aroused and generally anxious, you may wish to begin by using relaxation or self-hypnosis to lower your general level of arousal. In addition, learn to use the techniques described in Chapter 8 to help yourself cope with anxiety attacks. You must be sure that you understand what to do if you experience an attack of anxiety, because anxiety attacks will probably continue for some time after you have begun to deal with your agoraphobia. (They have, after all, become a habit, and so can easily be sparked off.) Ensure, therefore, that you know how to cope without escaping from the scene of an anxiety attack; if you do escape, you will ultimately strengthen your phobia.

Treatment for the phobia itself is based on the desensitisation method described earlier. First of all, establish a hierarchy of situations and locations which you fear at the moment. Start with the least frightening and work upwards. You should spend time and effort on this, so that the finished hierarchy is accurate. It might look like this:

1. standing on the front door step
2. walking to the garden gate
3. walking 10 feet down the pavement
4. walking 10 yards down the pavement
5. walking to the end of the road
6. walking or riding into town
7. sitting in the town centre
8. stepping just inside the doors of a shop

9. spending five minutes right inside the shop
10. sitting in a cinema near the door
11. sitting in a cinema in the centre of a row
12. going to a public lecture or discussion
13. going to a party with many other people, and so on

You must be able to relax and imagine yourself in the different situations on your hierarchy. Remember to go through it only as fast as you are able while remaining deeply relaxed. Practise this technique frequently – at least twice a day – until you are satisfied with your achievement. The final stage is to go through your desensitisation hierarchy for real. At first you may wish to have someone with you, but your ultimate aim should be to move outside independently.

ANOTHER APPROACH TO PHOBIA

All phobias can be treated with the desensitisation techniques described above. However, there are many other methods – most of which really require the assistance of a professional. For example, a phobic individual may be asked to relax and encouraged to visualise his most anxiety-provoking situation in vivid detail until the scene loses its terrors for him and simply becomes boring. This may take anything up to two hours. The method is known as 'implosion'.

REFERENCES

Eysenck, H. J. (1977). *You and Neurosis*, pp. 70–1. Maurice Temple Smith, London.

Hauck, P. (1981). *Why Be Afraid*, pp. 11–12. Sheldon Press, London.

Melville, J. (1977). *Phobias and Obsessions*, p. 125. George Allen and Unwin, London.

Watts, C. A. H. (1973). *Depression: The Blue Plague*, p. 80. Priory Press, London.

10. Worried Thinking

Anxiety is made up of two major components: *emotionality* and *worry*. Emotionality is the combination of emotional feelings and physical symptoms which we have already discussed. Worry, on the other hand, is a cognitive or thinking process. Woolfolk and Richardson (1979) put it neatly:

> Behind the health-disrupting symptoms of anxiety is usually found a very personal kind of worried, fearful thinking. It may take the form of feverish or panicky worry about some imminent personal disaster. Or it may be painful rumination about social or work performances that do not meet up to one's own or others' standards. Or perhaps it is sombre tense plotting and replotting of ways to surmount obstacles to goals one feels must not fail to reach. At the core of anxiety, though, is worry – worry about social and financial disasters, worry about loss of self-esteem, worry about failing to reach one's goals, worry about emotional and material security in an uncertain world. Worry, especially chronic or repetitious worry, produces fearful moods, physical tension, and all the other symptoms of anxiety.

But what *is* worry? Chiefly, it is the way one thinks about a situation. Perhaps most people do not realise that this has a significant effect on the extent of one's anxiety. Therefore, before we go any further, let us consider some examples of the more obvious kind of worried thoughts which people might have in different situations.

1. *A student anxious about the exam he is taking*: Look at that question! It's harder than I thought. I studied the whole subject and I can't remember anything about it . . . What's *wrong* with

me? Why can't I think straight? Every time I take an exam, the same thing happens . . . What if I fail?

Or: Oh no! Anything but that subject! I never could understand it. What on earth do they want? I just don't know what to do. Now I'm running out of time . . . Oh God, I feel sick. This is the end!

2. *A woman anxious about her financial situation*: Another large bill! I don't know where I'm going to find the money to pay it. And what will John say when he sees it? He was furious last week when the phone bill arrived. And then there's the car due to go in for its service next week. We must have that done. But all this money going out doesn't seem to leave enough to live on . . . I'll have to discuss it with John, but he hates talking about it . . . Oh, whatever am I going to do?

3. *A businessman*: Things just aren't going right for me. Everything I touch seems to fall apart. What if that contract with Johnson's falls through? That would be the last straw. I'm sure they're all beginning to think the company could do without me. Suppose I was fired? What then? I'd better try even harder . . .

We could go on multiplying examples for ever, but the ones above have illustrated the point adequately. In each of those cases, the people concerned were 'talking' to themselves about the situation in a negative way. This kind of *negative self-talk*, and worried thinking in general, seem to have several distinct characteristics, no matter where or when they occur. These are: (a) self-criticism, (b) expectation of failure, (c) thoughts about the consequences of failure, (d) escalating worry, (e) self-directed attention, and (f) inability to choose between alternatives. We shall briefly consider these in the order they are listed.

(a) *Self-criticism* and self-condemnation are extremely common. They take the form of calling oneself names such as 'stupid' or addressing oneself something like this: 'You made a right mess of that, didn't you?' In part, this way of thinking reflects a poor self-esteem (see Chapter 11).

(b) *Expectation of failure* is the natural result of failing many times before. For example, a shy person may be unable or unwilling to meet and speak to people in a social setting. Instead, he 'escapes' from the situation and feels a tremendous surge of relief. Of course, this sense of relief simply makes him more likely to avoid similar situations in the future. Indirectly, it also reinforces his belief that he is unable to cope with such events, so that next time a similar situation arises, he feels inadequate, depressed, useless – a failure. He thinks: 'I couldn't do it before; I can't do it now.' If he believes that, then that is how things will be.

(c) *Thoughts about the consequences of failure* can be very distressing indeed. The anxious person knows all the reasons why he should take a particular course of action or why he needs to succeed, yet his anxiety prevents him from doing so. And the situation is made worse because he may desperately want to succeed. Think of a student sitting an exam which he knows is vital to his career. He is probably slightly anxious before he starts, and because of this, any difficulty with the first few questions may make him worry about the later questions. He may even begin to imagine being unable to complete the examination, and then start to torture himself with thoughts of failure and the shame and humiliation which he believes would follow.

(d) *Escalating* worry means literally what it suggests: that worried thoughts do not occur singly – they multiply, and once one has set in, others rapidly follow. Dr Paul Hauck uses the word 'catastrophise' to refer to this process. And he is exactly right, for that word emphasises how worried thoughts can make a situation appear to be far worse than it actually is. For example, many people become very anxious when they know they will have to meet others in a social situation. Yet despite the fact that their fears (which, incidentally, are usually rather vague) never seem to be justified, they continue to feel anxious on similar occasions in the future. One of the reasons for this is that they worry about the worst possibilities. This tendency stems from the fact that when you meet other people you do not usually know whether they will like or accept you. If you are a worrier, you then begin to 'catastrophise'. You think of the things that might happen. You *might*, for example, be humiliated or embarrassed, or you *might* seem ignorant or be unable to speak confidently. This makes you dread the situation and so you begin to try and work out all the possibilities, or to plan what you might have to say so you won't be embarrassed. And before you know it, you're thinking you're the most inept, awkward person in the whole world and you're going to meet someone much smarter than yourself. After that, is it any wonder that you're so nervous when you meet other ordinary people?

(e) *Self-directed attention* suggests that an anxious person not only thinks in the wrong way, but that he also thinks about the wrong things. In earlier chapters of this book we explained how an anxious individual tends to concentrate on his emotional and physical feelings rather than on the task in hand. It may now be obvious to you that an anxious person also concentrates on his worries about an event or situation rather than on the event or situation itself. Clearly there is a major difference between task-directed and self-directed attention. You can see how two students of equal intelligence may achieve vastly different results as a direct consequence of the way they direct their attention under exam conditions. One focuses on his task: he thinks calmly and rationally about the best way to plan his time and his answers. The other focuses on his own thoughts and feelings: he may start well enough, but at some point he begins to worry about his answers, or about the fact that his hands are sweating, or whatever, and he becomes more and more anxious. For example, if he becomes aware of his physical tension, he may become even more tense in his efforts to 'fight it'. As we have seen, this will only make matters worse. And with only part of his attention directed to dealing with the exam, his performance will inevitably suffer.

(f) *The inability to choose between alternatives* is a natural result of one's mind being preoccupied with worried thoughts. Any anxious person finds that his ability to think clearly is diminished. He may also be unable to distinguish between trivia and essential matters, so that he spends time trying to make what is, in reality, a simple decision or choice between two or more alternatives.

WHY WORRY?

We have now listed the more important and obvious characteristics of worried thinking, but we have not yet considered why some people worry more than others. In fact there is a simple enough answer to this problem: a person thinks in a worried way because he believes – either consciously or subconsciously – that worry is useful. This may seem to be a strange statement, but your own experience may bear it out. Sometimes, in among the worried thoughts passing through your mind, you may notice the suspicion that worry is unproductive. Yet you never take any notice of this thought – you simply carry on worrying. Why? Surely the answer must be that you do not feel secure unless you are worrying? In other words, you believe that you can avoid unpleasant events or situations in the future by worrying *now*.

Unfortunately this is quite wrong. And a person who believes it, has mistaken worry for calm, rational planning and evaluation of a situation. To start with, worry itself gives you a distorted perception of any situation: you see it as worse than it really is. More importantly, however, excessive concern with short-term problems can obscure more significant events in the future. And, of course, no matter how much one may worry, one can never take account of any unexpected events which may occur.

Woolfolk and Richardson (1979) have emphasised the difference between calm, rational planning and frenzied, unproductive, anxiety-making worry. They have done this by pointing out that every event in the future must fall into either of two categories: the first made up of events which we can influence in some way; the second made up of events which we cannot influence at all. (Of course, some events move from one category to the other as circumstances change, and sometimes we can only influence certain aspects of a situation. But, basically, all future events fall into one or other of these two categories.)

Firstly, consider those events which one *can* influence in some way. If you accept that you have some degree of control over future events, then you must also accept that the only way of exercising that control is to *act*. Sitting back and worrying, endlessly tossing aside one idea after another, will achieve nothing. However, rationally planning how to control events, and then putting those plans into effect, can achieve everything! Furthermore, once you have taken action, worrying about whether or not your plans will work is pointless – either they will or they won't. But if you still feel concerned, you can go on to plan (a) what to do if your plans work and (b) what to do if your plans don't work. This is much more productive than worrying, which tends to obscure the real issues and can be emotionally exhausting.

What, then, of the second group of events – those which one cannot influence? In this case, worry is even more futile. For if you *do not* know what will happen in the future, worrying is only going to make you think about all the negative and unpleasant possibilities (which are probably very unlikely to happen anyway). Nor do you have any reason to worry if you *do* know what will happen in the future, because you can, if necessary, make suitable plans in advance.

Planning may not be easy if you have had a tendency to worry in the past. It involves collecting all the information relevant to a problem, working out the possible consequences of different courses of action, and then deciding what to do.

One particularly interesting point about worried thinking is that it can lead to procrastination and so give the appearance of laziness. A worried person may put off decisions or actions until the last possible moment, because it is often preferable to delay facing a problem rather than experience the worry associated with thinking about that problem. Of course, such short-term considerations can give rise to even greater problems in the future.

It is difficult to make a worried person see the utter futility of his way of thinking. Here are some points which may help *you* to gain sight of the futility of worry:

- first and foremost, worry causes stress and anxiety
- no amount of worry will change a single thing
- worry prevents you enjoying a present moment, 'here and now' existence because you're concentrating on the future
- worry prevents you facing up to reality (which can of course be very useful if you don't want to)

Besides reasoning things out, there are other ways you can help yourself to stop worrying. You may find it helpful to incorporate an appropriate suggestion into the self-hypnosis techniques described in Chapter 4. One such suggestion for the tape recorder technique might be: 'You find that you are worrying less and less often, less and less severely, all the time now.' You could also include specific suggestions to help yourself overcome any especially troublesome worries. Another useful idea is simply to say forcefully or think the words 'STOP IT' whenever you catch yourself worrying – no matter how many times a day this may be. A third idea is to examine your basic beliefs and assumptions and adjust those which are the cause of your worry. We introduced this subject in Chapter 2 and shall return to it in Chapter 11.

As you become more aware of, and sensitive to, the worried thoughts which pass through your mind, you will begin to notice that they are not all at an overt, conscious level. Much, if not most, of our worried thinking continues whether our full attention is focused on it or not. So if you experience the symptoms of stress and anxiety, but you don't know why, you may find it helpful to analyse the way you think about people, events and situations. If you realise you have a habit of worrying, you can then begin to deal effectively with it.

REPLACING NEGATIVE SELF-TALK WITH POSITIVE SELF-TALK

Perhaps the most important method of stopping worried thoughts is to replace your negative self-talk with calm and realistic positive self-talk. There are three steps in this procedure: identification, decision and substitution.

Identification involves making yourself aware of your negative mental statements, thoughts and images. There are three main ways in which you can do this. Firstly, by thinking back to occasions when you have been anxious or worried in the past, and recalling what you thought to yourself at that time. Secondly, by simply noting down what you think at the times you are anxious or worried (or as soon afterwards as possible). Thirdly, by relaxing and vividly imagining an anxiety-producing situation as though you are actually a part of it and then taking note of whatever thoughts come to mind.

Decision is the process of making a resolution to stop thinking negatively. As with any other self-help procedure, it is no use vaguely considering how much you would like to think positively. Your commitment to the idea must be firm, or you will simply not have enough determination to carry the procedure through to completion.

Substitution is the process of replacing your negative thoughts with positive ones. However, you must ensure that your positive statements are *realistic*. As an illustration of this, consider the following example. Here are three self-statements typical of a person who has difficulty being assertive:

1. 'I can never get what I want.'
2. 'Every time I try to put forward my point of view, I become anxious and confused.'
3. 'What's the point of saying anything? Nobody ever listens to me.'

He might try to replace these statements with unrealistic ones such as:

1. 'I am definitely going to get my own way this time.'
2. 'I am going to remain completely calm and relaxed.'
3. 'I will make my opinions known to everyone.'

These statements are unrealistic because they represent a dramatic change from this person's previous patterns of behaviour. Quite simply, his existing anxiety will prevent him from fulfilling them. And he will then see himself as having failed yet again – which will make him feel even worse! He should try to cultivate more realistic statements such as these:

1. 'No-one can expect to get what they want all the time. Even so, I have a right to expect others to acknowledge my wishes. If they refuse to do so, then I shall make it clear that I am dissatisfied and that I want to know exactly why I have been ignored.'
2. 'I realise that I may well feel slightly anxious when I present my case. This does not mean that I will necessarily get confused and forget what I am saying. I will just accept any feelings of nervousness, without getting tense or worried, and continue as best I can.'
3. 'Certainly not everyone will want to hear what I have to say. But I shall try to ensure that I give myself the best possible chance of being heard. So it will help if I plan what I want to say before I actually stand up to speak. Then I shall present

my arguments as clearly and concisely as possible. This may be difficult, but it will seem easier if I remember how important it is to me that I do not give up yet again.'

We can conclude this chapter by listing three of the most common types of worry associated with anxiety:

1. *Worries about time* with negative self-talk such as: 'I must hurry', 'What if I don't finish on time?', and so on. Positive statements to replace these might include: 'Take things calmly! One step at a time', 'You can only work at a certain speed', 'Don't worry about problems before they occur. Just start the job and get on with it.'

2. *Worries about personal ability* with negative self-talk such as: 'I'm so stupid', 'I'm never going to be able to do this', 'I hate myself', and so on. Positive statements to replace these might include: 'I know I can do it, and that's what counts', 'I do have the ability to complete this job', 'I can and I will.'

3. *Worries about the way one feels* with negative self-talk such as: 'Why do I feel like this?', 'I'm so confused I can't decide what to do!', 'Oh no! that migraine/indigestion/tension is here again! What can I do?' Positive statements to replace these might include: 'It's only natural to feel some tension in this situation', 'I will take a short break and return when my mind is fresh.'

REFERENCE

Woolfolk, R. L. and Richardson, F. C. (1979). *Stress, Sanity and Survival*, p. 44. Futura, London.

11. Understanding Social Anxiety

As we explained in Chapter 7, most people experience a certain amount of anxiety before or during objectively harmless situations which involve (social) contact with other men and women. In fact, this is such a common experience that we can consider it to be 'normal'. Sometimes, however, this anxiety grows to a point where an individual feels reluctant to enter the situation which causes it. In this chapter, we shall make some suggestions about the causes of anxiety like this. And because such 'social' anxiety often occurs against a background of personality characteristics such as feelings of inferiority, a lack of self-confidence, poor self-esteem, and so forth, we shall also examine those problems in this chapter.

Research has shown that social anxiety (or, as we often say, shyness) manifests itself in three main ways: the symptoms of anxiety itself, such as a pounding heart or blushing; the behaviour which results from the anxiety, such as a reluctance to talk to others (reticence); and intense feelings of embarrassment or self-consciousness. Perhaps we should emphasise that although some people are permanently and chronically shy, others only experience anxiety in a few specific situations. Thus, for example, you may be quite relaxed when meeting people in the course of your work, but find it an ordeal to meet a group of strangers at a party.

The first question to answer when discussing this subject is: *how* and *why* does this kind of anxiety and shyness develop? This question has no simple answer, for it can be approached from many different angles. Some psychologists believe that the cause is simple conditioning from unpleasant past experience. Psychoanalysts, on the other hand, believe that the cause lies in the emotional traumas and life experience of early childhood.

And a third group of psychologists claim that such anxiety is a result of the way we perceive the world around us. Let us now see how these factors might contribute to a person's anxiety in dealing with others.

Our first example centres on the process of conditioning, a term we first explained on page 101. To recap, an unpleasant experience which produces anxiety can 'condition' us to feel anxious in similar situations in the future. The series of events involved in this process is illustrated by the experiences of a young man called Paul, who had recently left school. He was initially very confident when applying for employment, but at his second interview he made a serious mistake which confused and embarrassed him. He 'made a mess' of the rest of this interview but afterwards thought 'that was the end of the matter'. However, before his next interview he discovered he felt very anxious and began to wonder if the same thing would happen again. With each successive interview, his performance worsened and his anxiety increased. Finally, matters came to a head. In his words: 'I knew I just couldn't face it. When the receptionist called out my name, I panicked – and fled the building!'

This series of events is typical of a conditioned anxiety response: the mounting anxiety, the decrease in performance, the worry, the desire to 'escape' from the feared situation, the tremendous feeling of relief which escape produces, and so on. Indeed this outline can obviously be applied to many other situations of one sort or another.

However, conditioning is not a complete explanation of the origin of shyness and social anxiety. For example, why does the same event produce different degrees of anxiety in different individuals? The answer to this question must be that different people perceive the same event in different ways. You will recall that the type of events and situations which we are discussing here do not really pose an objective threat to our well-being. Rather, they induce anxiety because *we see in them a threat to our emotional well-being or self-esteem*. This idea implies that it is our perception of the possible outcome or consequences of an event, rather than the event itself, which produces anxiety. This leads us into the question: 'What possible outcome(s) of an event could cause such anxiety that a person comes to fear the event itself?' The answers would seem to be 'failure' and 'rejection'.

THE FEAR OF FAILURE AND THE FEAR OF REJECTION

There is good reason to suppose that a great deal of social anxiety and shyness stems from these two basic fears. 'Failure' means failure (for whatever reason) to live up to your own standards or to fulfil your own expectations of yourself. 'Rejection' means any response from another person which you perceive as an expression of rejection of you as an individual, and may include anything from mild criticism to outright hostility and condemnation. Even something as harmless as a disapproving look might be interpreted as rejection by a very sensitive person.

Obviously these fears are not always overt – they may be subconscious rather than conscious. But if you consider this idea for a moment, you will see that it is indeed possible to interpret many anxiety-provoking situations in terms of one or both of these two fears. For example, you may be reluctant to ask someone of the opposite sex for a date because you are worried about the possibility that he or she will say 'no' – which is, in a sense, a rejection (or at least can be interpreted that way). Or you may be reluctant to meet people at a party because you believe they might be better dressed or better educated or more socially adept or more intelligent than you. If you believe this, you may easily begin to worry about whether or not they will wish to speak to you ('rejection' again), or alternatively whether or not you will fail in your efforts to speak to them. You may feel anxious at an interview because you believe that you are likely to perform badly – in other words, to fail. Similar reasoning can be applied to innumerable other situations: interpersonal exchanges, confrontations, working to deadlines, making a speech, and so on. The possibilities are endless.

If we accept that the fear of failure and the fear of rejection are at the root of at least some specific anxieties, we need to consider why people actually 'fear' failure and rejection – and also why different individuals do so to different extents. The explanation lies in the nature of *self-esteem*, that is, roughly, the opinion one holds of oneself, or one's evaluation of one's own worth as a person.

SELF-ESTEEM

People do not generally give much conscious thought to their opinion of themselves. However, in times of stress or in difficult circumstances, a person may begin to think such thoughts as these: 'I hate myself.' 'I can't do anything right.' 'Oh, what's the use? I'll never be able to do it.'

Thoughts like these are closely associated with a poor self-esteem – a low opinion of oneself. Now, a poor self-esteem tends to be associated with feelings of depression, anxiety and inadequacy; it follows that a loss of self-esteem may cause a person to become depressed. This means that someone with a poor self-esteem will tend to experience feelings of depression and anxiety more often and to a greater extent than someone with a stronger sense of self-worth. In addition, he or she will try to avoid any situation which could adversely affect his or her self-esteem. And the most obvious types of situation in which a loss of self-esteem can occur are those which involve failure and rejection. (We do not mean to suggest that everyone interprets failure and rejection as a reflection on their sense of self-worth; but many people do.)

We have now reached a point at which we need to examine the factors that determine a person's self-esteem.

SELF-IMAGE AND SELF-ESTEEM

Your self-image is the total of all the impressions which you have of yourself. It is built up of your impressions about your body, age, sex, intelligence, personal ability, personality traits, job, achievements and so on, and also how you *feel* about those impressions.

In addition to your self-image, you will have an image of a set of ideal characteristics: the ones which you would choose for yourself, were it possible to do so. These characteristics make up what is called your 'ideal self'. It tends to be based on real or imagined people whom you envy or admire.

As you probably realise, there is usually a discrepancy between a person's self-image and his or her ideal self: the smaller this discrepancy, the happier he or she will be. In fact the size of this discrepancy is a rough measure of a person's self-esteem. Thus someone with a large discrepancy between his or her self-image and ideal self will tend to have a poor self-esteem.

It is extremely important to remember that there may be an objectively real difference between your ideal self and your self-image. On the other hand, your self-image may be based on your own wildly inaccurate perceptions and beliefs about yourself. Depending on the nature of these inaccurate perceptions (do you see yourself in a favourable or an unfavourable way?), the gap between your self-image and ideal self may be either smaller or greater in your mind than in reality.

Bearing this fact in mind, it may be useful to mention briefly some of the psychological techniques which a person can use to stabilise his self-image. These include:

1. *Selective interaction*: he associates only with people who behave in a similar way to himself, or with those people whom he knows will reinforce his self-image (which, incidentally, is one reason why shy people often have a small circle of a few close friends).
2. *Defence mechanisms*: for example, he may disregard, discredit or misinterpret the unfavourable reactions of others towards his speech or actions (because if he were to accept those reactions as appropriate, he might be forced to re-evaluate his self-image).
3. *Selective evaluation of self*: in other words, he ignores aspects of his own behaviour, appearance or personality which contradict his self-image.
4. *Response evocation*: that is, he behaves in a way that evokes from other people the sort of responses which will reinforce his self-image.

Psychological and behavioural techniques like these, which can help to stabilise and justify one's self-image, are very important, because we tend to feel anxious and depressed when our self-image is threatened. And of course the anxiety and depression increase in proportion to the importance which we attach to the part of our overall self-image which is threatened.

EXPECTATIONS AND SELF-IMAGE

Our self-image has a major effect on the way we behave and act in any situation. For example, if you perceive yourself as a poor conversationalist or an unassertive person, you probably have difficulty in speaking to people or in asserting yourself. If you believe you are attractive, you probably behave as if you expect to be accepted; if you believe you are unattractive, perhaps you behave as if you expect to be 'rejected'. But no matter what you expect, people usually respond accordingly. However, research has shown that we actually use other people's reactions to our behaviour as confirmation that our self-image is correct! Thus changing the way you see yourself can be a major step to altering both your behaviour and people's reactions to you. We shall see how it is possible to change one's self-image by using visualisation techniques later in the chapter.

Of course, our expectations are not limited to the examples described above. We all hold expectations about every single aspect of our lives. For example, you will have a set of expectations about the behaviour and attitudes of your wife or husband, your personal friends, your colleagues at work, and so forth. And within each area of expectations, you will hold what can be described as negative and positive expectations. For example:

What you expect from yourself
  positive – intelligence, aptitude, determination, tolerance and so on
  negative – stupidity, ineptitude, lack of persistence, lack of tolerance and so on.

What you expect from life
  positive – good rewards, fair play, recognition of your individuality and so on
  negative – to be cheated, downtrodden, abused and so on

As we have already suggested, a person's self-image and expectations are closely linked. For example, a man who expects to succeed at his job, gain promotion and obtain high financial rewards may have an image of himself as intelligent, confident, successful and skilful in business. It is not difficult to see why a person with so many positive expectations and such a strong self-image will almost certainly have a high self-esteem. Nor is it difficult to see why people with many negative expectations about life, relationships and the world in general tend to have a poor self-image and a low self-esteem.

ANXIETY CAUSED BY THREATS TO EXPECTATIONS AND SELF-IMAGE

We are now in a position to consider in more detail the ways in which threats to one's expectations or self-image can produce anxiety and depression. These are:

- *Threats to positive expectations*: if you hold a number of positive expectations to which you attach great importance (such as obtaining a job, pulling off a business deal, gaining promotion, establishing and maintaining a relationship, obtaining respect from your children), and these expectations are not fulfilled or are placed at risk, or even if you worry about the possibility that they will not be fulfilled, you may develop anxiety.
- *Holding negative expectations*: any negative expectation which you hold will predispose you to feel anxious and depressed, because of the way in which negative expectations can reduce your self-esteem.
- *Threats to self-image*: any situation which might affect your self-image in such a way that your self-esteem is reduced will produce anxiety (and depression if the reduction of self-esteem actually takes place).

FEELINGS OF INFERIORITY

Such feelings – which seem to be extremely common – stem from the perception that the people around you possess the characteristics of your ideal self, while you do not. These perceptions can cause a great deal of anguish and anxiety. (In passing, let us note that the term 'inferiority complex' refers to a particular form of behaviour shown by those individuals who have basic feelings of inferiority, but who behave over-confidently and exuberantly in an attempt to compensate.) Generally, feelings of inferiority involve a poor self-esteem, feelings of depression, and critical thoughts and feelings about one's abilities, appearance and other personal qualities. We shall return to this problem later in the chapter.

SELF-CONFIDENCE

Although it is hard to define exactly what is meant by this expression, it seems that we judge other people's self-confidence from a mixture of personality characteristics, including self-assertiveness, emotionality of response to difficult situations, level of self-esteem and so on. In addition, a person's expectations about the outcome of any situation, based on his own past experience, must contribute to his estimation of his own level of self-confidence. Thus, for example, a person who has failed to achieve what he desires many times in the past will have many negative expectations about his chance of success in the future – and will feel that he lacks self-confidence. We should also bear in mind that emotional problems can reduce one's ability to make decisions: this may appear as a lack of confidence in one's own judgement. We shall consider some ways in which a person can increase his or her self-confidence later in the chapter.

REDUCING SOCIAL ANXIETY, IMPROVING YOUR SELF-IMAGE AND BOOSTING SELF-CONFIDENCE

CONTROLLING ANXIETY

In addition to the techniques described below, the techniques described in Chapters 4, 8 and 10 are all helpful in developing your ability to control feelings of anxiety. So as you read this chapter, please remember that it does not stand in isolation from the rest of the book.

UNDERSTANDING SOCIAL ANXIETY

CHANGING NEGATIVE BELIEFS AND PERCEPTIONS ABOUT YOURSELF

Many people's thoughts, beliefs and perceptions about themselves are, at least to some degree, inaccurate or distorted. Yet even if you perceive yourself in a way that is distorted by misconceptions and assumptions that are quite wrong, those perceptions still have a major effect on how you think and behave in many situations. Thus analysing your basic beliefs and checking their relevance and accuracy can be a significant step towards a reduction of the stress which produces emotional distress. (Earlier in this chapter, we explained that anxiety and depression tend to develop when any important part of one's self-image is threatened. However, this does not mean that a realistic evaluation and appraisal of the beliefs and perceptions which you hold about yourself need be threatening. For, if carried out correctly, such an evaluation can provide a firm basis for the modification of parts of your self-image which are inherently weak or incorrect.)

However, before you can analyse the beliefs which you hold about yourself, it is necessary to identify them. How can this be done? First of all, let us emphasise that we are not concerned here with major life crises or changes, but with the smaller, unavoidable, repeated stresses of life which act as a source of stress, worry and anxiety. Woolfolk and Richardson (1979) have observed that two infallible indicators of stress are '(1) worried anticipation of future events that cannot be avoided, and (2) being preoccupied with and ruminating about these events for a period of time after they occur'. So by using these two criteria, you can identify and list the situations which, for you, produce stress, anxiety, worry and perhaps depression.

Suppose that you have identified certain types of situations which cause you to feel stressed. You may recall from Chapter 1 that a situation itself cannot cause stress – rather, it is your perception of, and reaction to, any situation which is the crucial factor in emotional disturbance. Now, your reaction to a situation depends to a large extent on the beliefs and assumptions which you hold about that situation and about how it affects you. Those beliefs and assumptions can be brought into conscious focus in two main ways:

1. By asking yourself questions about the situation, for example:

'What is it about this situation that I find stressful?'
'Does the situation objectively justify my emotional reaction?'
'Am I reacting this way from habit?'
'Is the whole situation stressful, or only part of it?'
2. By identifying clues in the way you think and speak to yourself and others about a situation, that is, identifying the cause of your stress from your 'self-talk' (see Chapter 10).

Once you have identified the beliefs which make any situation stressful, you can begin to change them. To illustrate this process, let us take the example of a man who feels anxious and shy in social situations. First of all, he carefully considers the cause of his anxiety. By doing so, he comes to realise that his anxiety stems from the belief that other people don't want to know him, or to have him in their circle of friends, because he lacks some particular characteristic (this will vary from person to person – it might be social ability, charm, intelligence and so on).

Next, he decides to replace this faulty belief with a more realistic and less stress-producing one. Let us suppose that he decided on the following: 'I can develop whatever ability and skills may be necessary to achieve the things I really desire. I have the potential to get on well with others, even if I sense they do not like me, and I can accept this without feeling rejected or less of a person. I can learn to love myself.'

The third step is for him to consider how his new belief will alter his thoughts, feelings and behaviour. Here are some examples of the sort of changes he might expect to achieve, set out in his own words.

1. To be more relaxed in the company of others; no longer constantly comparing myself with them or criticising my failure to match up to what I see as their standards; to stop calling myself 'stupid' or 'foolish'; to accept my mistakes more easily.
2. Less introspection and self-analysis, and more constructive action. Stop seeing references to myself in other people's actions.
3. Be able to tackle specific problems more easily and to take the initiative in calling up others; to greet friends in a relaxed way and stop worrying about what I do or say.

UNDERSTANDING SOCIAL ANXIETY

4. To treat other people more as equals; to enjoy social occasions for what they are, and to return invitations in a relaxed way.

(Based on Woolfolk and Richardson, 1979)

Changing beliefs like this can be difficult. We all hold many inaccurate beliefs, either because we have simply never questioned them or because they have some personal value (for example, many of our incorrect beliefs reinforce our self-images and thereby maintain our self-esteem). Therefore you must criticise, question and think through each of the beliefs which cause you to feel stressed or to react emotionally to events around you. You will then be able to decide whether each belief is valid – or whether it should be discarded and replaced with another, more reasonable, one. Even so, such self-analysis and careful thought are not enough. To quote Woolfolk and Richardson once again: 'It is harder to think yourself into a new way of acting than it is to act yourself into a new way of thinking.' Thus each time you question or criticise one of your beliefs and replace it with another, you should act – act in a way that will reinforce both the reality of, and your acceptance of, your new attitude and belief.

Such action may be difficult. For example, a shy person may find it difficult to go out and meet other people. But this is essential, for otherwise change cannot become a reality. You may find it helpful to remember that an action is often more useful done badly than not done at all! (Do you believe that you must do everything well? If so, why?) And of course experience will improve your skill at any action. We shall return to this point in a moment.

It would be quite impossible to list every belief which causes stress and emotional distress. Rather, we shall examine some of the major categories of belief which contribute to stress and personal problems.

1. *Believing that you cannot change the way you act and feel.* A surprising number of people fail to accept the responsibility of self-change – no matter how unhappy they are. They present excuses for this attitude such as: 'I've always been this way' and 'That's just how I am.' But such beliefs are quite wrong. Change *is* possible, using the techniques

described here, with or without professional help. If you find that you have adopted a similar attitude, perhaps you should give serious consideration to the possibility that you *don't want to change*. That is a matter for you alone to decide. (In recent years, there has been much discussion of the role which our parents and other early influences have on our actions later in life. And it does seem that we all tend to believe many things which we learned or were told as children without ever questioning them. However, you now have an autonomous adult ego, and you can use it to work things out for yourself. So don't just make statements like 'That's the way things are' – check them out. To repeat what we said earlier, *you* are running *your* life and *you* have the ability – and the right – to decide what to do with it.)

2. *Believing that your life is controlled by events in the world around you, and that other people make you act as you do*. These two beliefs are closely related to number 1 above. In actual fact, most people's lives probably *are* controlled to a large extent by what goes on around them. And it is not hard to see why. Unless a person makes firm decisions about the course he wishes his life to take, and then begins to act in a way that will bring his plans to fruition, he will inevitably be buffeted about by circumstances beyond his control.

Fortunately, one can learn to control one's life – at least to a much greater extent than many of us do at the moment. What of the belief that other people make you act as you do? A moment's thought reveals how misguided this belief actually is. For example, you may make, and believe, statements such as: 'He made me so angry.' 'Now see what you made me do!' But this is ridiculous. You respond to events around you with anger, for example, because in some way you believe that anger is the correct or appropriate response. You say that other people 'made' you do something because that is how you perceive the situation – not because it really is like that. In reality, we can all learn to control our lives and our behaviour and our actions – even though it may take time.

3. *Believing that the way you see yourself is correct, when in fact it is not*. You may perceive yourself as possessing more or less attributes than you have in reality. In either case, if an

UNDERSTANDING SOCIAL ANXIETY

event or situation challenges your self-image, you may experience depression or anxiety. Yet it is extremely difficult to see through the personal beliefs, attitudes and prejudices which contribute to an inaccurate self-image. And it is extremely difficult to ask for – or obtain – unbiased, objective, helpful guidance from other people. One way of overcoming these difficulties is to spend a few minutes each day quietly reflecting on how you behaved, how you would like to have behaved, and what part of your behaviour caused you to feel stressed, during the events of the day. This kind of 'debriefing' can be extremely helpful in providing a focus for self-change. But don't let it become obsessive.

4. *Believing that you are inferior to other people.* Feelings of inferiority are extremely common; indeed they are probably one of the most common sources of emotional distress in our society. Feelings of inferiority may start as a perceived inferiority or disadvantage in one area of life or personality (a lack of charm, good looks, education, intelligence, social ability and so on) which then generalises to a vague feeling of inferiority to the world in general. Yet most psychiatrists would tell you that although the majority of people think their moments of self-doubt, their innermost secrets and desires, their emotional experiences and behaviour, are unique to them, in reality we are all basically the same. Of course, we all have different personal attributes and success in life, but it is also a fact that for any particular personal ability or attribute, we are all inferior to some people and superior to others. You must remember that social status, education, upbringing and so on do not indicate a person's innate 'value' – even if society tends to adopt that attitude. There are many other more praiseworthy qualities: sincerity, loyalty, honesty, affection, to name just a few. You should also remember that even the people you envy and admire do not lead perfectly harmonious lives – in fact, everyone has basically the same human problems. Finally, trying to make yourself into something you are not, in order to overcome feelings of inferiority and 'compete' on an equal level, is futile. Although taking greater care of your appearance, improving your knowledge and social skills, and so on, obviously help to increase self-confidence, the real cure for feelings of inferiority is to decide

that you are not inferior but are equal, and to overcome the beliefs which stand between you and happiness.
5. *Believing that you must do everything as near perfectly as possible.* This belief has been called 'the curse of perfectionism'. It prevents you from obtaining satisfaction or fulfilment from what you do; it causes you constantly to examine and recheck your actions, it makes you feel a failure if you achieve less than perfection. Anyone with this problem needs to learn to relax, take pleasure in his achievements, and enjoy life more.
6. *Believing that failure reflects on you as an individual.* We have already explained that failure may lower a person's self-esteem. This is especially true when someone has learnt to judge his sense of self-worth by events outside himself – for example, by what he achieves or by material worth, status, respect from others, financial or business power. In such cases, failure to achieve something takes on a greater significance: in that person's mind, it implies he is 'no good', 'useless', 'a failure'. Such a person should remember that failure in what he does is not the same as failure as a person. Furthermore, one cannot compensate for a low self-esteem by achieving material worth or any of the other attributes mentioned above.
7. *Believing that your emotional security depends on a particular place or person.* Dependency is a major cause of stress. People, places and relationships change spontaneously, and such change can easily cause depression in a person who has located his emotional security in something outside himself. But in addition, the *threat* of change can cause separation anxiety and a loss of self-esteem. So remember in particular that being alone or *not* being in love only threaten your self-esteem and make you feel depressed if you are not sure of your own self-worth: hence the saying: 'You should learn to love yourself before you begin to love other people.' In passing we should also mention that the fear of rejection is closely related to a weak self-esteem and a high level of insecurity. To avoid the lowering of self-esteem which can result from rejection, a person may cut himself off completely from all the situations where rejection may occur. Hence a person may be isolated because he cannot handle his fear of rejection.

8. *Believing that worry is effective.* In Chapter 10, we explained that a person worries because he believes in some way that worry is effective and necessary. This is quite wrong. Worry is futile and emotionally exhausting.
9. *Believing that because you have failed before, you will fail again.* Research shows that we judge ourselves by other people's reactions to us. And, as we have already explained, the way we judge ourselves determines the way we behave. Thus a person may become entangled in a series of negative expectations about himself and his abilities, which directly determine the way he behaves. In the next section, we shall describe some ways in which these negative expectations can be defeated.

CHANGING YOUR SELF-IMAGE AND THE WAY YOU BEHAVE

On page 70, we mentioned that visualisation is a powerful tool for changing one's self-image. This is because visualisation can alter the way you see your own behaviour and also alter your expectations of the outcome of any situation.

To use these relaxation and visualisation techniques, you relax (see Chapter 3) and then, with your eyes shut, visualise yourself (that is, produce vivid mental imagery of yourself) taking part in each aspect of the events which currently produce anxiety. You may feel some anxiety as you go through the visualisation; if so, relax once more and then continue where you left off. Thus, for example, if you find it difficult to speak to members of the opposite sex, you might wish to visualise yourself in a scene in which you introduce yourself to someone and then talk to him or her in a relaxed way with no feelings of anxiety.

Once you have successfully visualised yourself coping adequately in a particular scene, relax once more. For a few minutes, do not think about the scene, but simply maintain a relaxed state of body and mind. Then return to the same scene and go through it in your imagination once again. You may feel some anxiety, but this should be less than before. Obviously your aim is to see yourself coping in the previously feared situation without any feelings of anxiety, therefore you should go through this cycle of visualisation and relaxation until that is what you have achieved. No matter what scene or situation you are visualising, make an effort to see yourself as an integral part of it, not just as though you are watching it as a detached observer. Sometimes it is useful to visualise a series of scenes, each one of which is currently more anxiety-provoking than the last. You can find more details on this hierarchical technique of desensitisation in Chapter 9.

An alternative approach is to prolong your visualisation until your anxiety begins to decrease of its own accord. If you adopt this technique, once again your aim should be to see yourself as a part of the situation. Imagine each part of the scene as you would like it to be; if your anxiety increases to an uncomfortable level, stop briefly and relax until it is under control. You may need to repeat your visualisation once or twice a day for several days until you feel confident of your ability to cope in the real situation.

Used correctly, these techniques have the power to change the way in which you perceive any situation, and also to modify your expectations of the way it will affect you. In other words, you begin to see yourself as able to cope; your self-image in relation to that situation is modified. However, as we mentioned before, thought alone is not enough: it needs to be followed up with action. This is a very important point. No matter what you fear, you will have to expose yourself to it before you can completely overcome your anxiety. For example, if you never attend an interview, you'll never be employed; if you never speak to a member of the opposite sex, you'll never get a date; if you never pluck up courage to speak to strangers, you'll never make new friends; and so on. In other words, you have everything to gain by turning your visualisation into reality.

However, this must be done in the correct way. Clearly it would be unreasonable to expect that you could cope with any situation, no matter how stressful, immediately. You must therefore set yourself realistic targets which will allow you to increase your confidence and overcome your anxiety gradually. Don't, for example, resolve that you will suddenly become the 'life and soul' of any social situation, but pick a more realistic goal, such as introducing yourself to two people each time you meet a group of strangers. Moreover, don't just make vague resolutions. Specify a time or date by which you will achieve your goal – and reward yourself in some way when you are successful (for example, see a film, buy yourself a new shirt or a bottle of wine, or do something you really enjoy). This kind of positive reinforcement can be of great value. At this point you may also wish to reread the section 'Don't set yourself up for failure', on pages 72–3. Much more information and many suggestions about goal-setting can be found in *The Success Factor* by Robert Sharpe and David Lewis, and *Shyness: What It Is and What to do About It* by Philip Zimbardo.

BOOSTING SELF-CONFIDENCE

There is some debate about the extent to which self-confidence is dependent on the possession of a comprehensive set of social skills. Zimbardo (1981) has suggested that there are two sorts of shy people: the first have a complete set of social skills but lack the confidence to use them; the second simply don't have a knowledge of social skills. In his book on shyness (mentioned above) he outlined a system for the development of social ability covering the following areas:

- developing a manner which attracts and holds other people's attention
- developing the confidence to approach feared situations by adopting a particular 'role'
- setting goals
- practising conversational skills, including: making introductions, initiating and maintaining a conversation, giving and accepting compliments, planning subjects about which you can talk knowledgeably, and ending a conversation or social meeting
- developing the ability to socialise freely and making friends from acquaintances
- handling interpersonal conflicts and becoming more assertive
- planning what to do in different situations

You may object to the idea that one can overcome anxiety by planning 'strategies' like these for use in social interactions. However, there is no doubt that a certain amount of forethought can considerably reduce worried anticipation and anxiety before any situation or event, in addition to controlling your negative expectations about the outcome of that event. If you feel that social skills are one of your weak points, such a programme may be very helpful.

We are, however, concerned here with a more direct approach to boosting self-confidence. This involves the use of the self-hypnosis systems described in Chapter 4. As we have done elsewhere in this book, we shall now outline a suggested approach for Stage 2 of the tape recorder technique:

> Your feelings of self-confidence are increasing all the time now. Each day you find your self-confidence is increasing, so that in business, at home or in social situations you are more relaxed and calm. You are more confident when talking to other people, more relaxed when you meet people new to you. These feelings of self-confidence are continuing to increase gradually as each day goes by. And as your self-confidence continues to increase, you find that you can successfully achieve those things which have made you feel anxious in the past. [If necessary:] And as your self-confidence increases, feelings of inferiority are troubling you less and less often, less and less severely all the time. Very soon they will have gone away completely.

Remember that there is no single correct way to be socially skilful. If you watch a group of people who seem socially adept, you will probably see that they all have different individual styles. Some are 'good listeners', while others will be witty conversationalists, and so on. You may find that by watching other people, you can model your own actions on the parts of their behaviour which seem most appropriate to you.

In conclusion, we emphasise once again one of the themes which has run through this whole book: ultimately, any change in any aspect of your personality can only occur if you wish it should do so – and if you then take appropriate action to make it occur.

REFERENCES

Sharpe, R. and Lewis, D. (1976). *The Success Factor*. Souvenir Press, London.

Woolfolk, R. L. and Richardson, F. C. (1979). *Stress, Sanity and Survival*. Futura Publications, London.

Zimbardo, P. (1981). *Shyness: What It Is and What to do About It*. Pan Books, London.

Further Reading

In addition to the titles included in the references at the end of the chapters the following is a short select list of books which might be helpful to individual readers. Of necessity it is selective and other titles will be found in Public Libraries, often under the section of 'Self-help'.

Benson, H. (1977). *The Relaxation Response*. Fount Paperbacks, London.
Cronin, D. (1980). *Anxiety, Depression and Phobias*. Granada, London.
Forsythe, E. (1978). *A Less Anxious You*. William Luscombe London.
Hurst-Vose, R. (1981). *Agoraphobia*. Faber and Faber, London.
Jacobson, E. (1977). *You Must Relax*. Souvenir Press, London.
Llewellyn-Jones, D. (1981). *Everyman*. Oxford University Press, Oxford.
Llewellyn-Jones, D. (1982). *Everywoman*, 3rd edition, Faber and Faber, London.
(Particularly useful for sexual and related information.)
Melville, J. (1977). *Phobias and Obsessions*. George Allen and Unwin, London.
Mitchell, L. (1977). *Simple Relaxation*. John Murray (Publishers) Ltd, London.
Norfolk, D. (1979). *The Stress Factor*. Hamlyn Books, London.
Selye, H. (1975). *Stress Without Distress*. Hodder and Stoughton, London.
Sharpe, R. and Lewis, D. (1979). *The Anxiety Antidote*. Souvenir Press, London.
Stanway, A. (1981). *Overcoming Depression*. Hamlyn Books, London.

Tyrer, P. (1980). *How to Cope with Stress*. Sheldon Press, London.
(Originally published as *Stress*.)

Watts, C. A. H. (1976). *Depression: The Blue Plague*, revised edition. Hodder and Stoughton, London.

Watts, C. A. H. (1980). *Defeating Depression: Guide for Depressed People and Their Families*. Thorsons, Wellingborough.

Useful Addresses

The following organisations are only a small selection of agencies which are available throughout the United Kingdom. For local self-help groups, contact the nearest Citizens Advice Bureau or Public Library.

British Association for Counselling
37a Sheep Street
Rugby CV21 3BX

British Society for Medical and Dental Hypnosis
42 Links Road
Ashtead
Surrey KT21 2HJ   Ashtead 73522

Open Door Assocation   (Self-help group for agoraphobics)
c/o 44 Pensby Road, Heswall
Merseyside L61 9PQ   051–648 2022

The Samaritans
Head Office: 17 Uxbridge Road
Slough SL1 1SH   Slough 32713
(See Yellow Page Directory for local offices)

Depressives Anonymous
83 Derby Road
Nottingham NG1 5BB

Depressives Associated
19 Merley Way
Wimbourne Minster, Dorset BH21 1QN   0202 883957

The Phobics Society
4 Cheltenham Road
Manchester M21 1QN   061–881 1937

MIND (National Association For Mental Health)
22 Harley Street
London W1N 2ED   01–491 2772

National Schizophrenia Fellowship
20 Victoria Road, Surbiton
Surrey KT6 4JT   01–390 3651

UNITED STATES OF AMERICA

American Society of Clinical Hypnosis
2250 E Devon Avenue
Des Plaines, IL 60018   (301) 231-9350

Emotions Anonymous
PO Box 4245
St Paul, MN 55104   (612) 647-9712

Neurotics Anonymous International Liaison
PO Box 4866, Cleveland Park Station
Washington, DC 20008   (202) 628-4379

Pass Group
(Panic Attack Sufferers' Support Group)
1042 E 105th Street
Brooklyn, NY 11236   (718) 763-0190

Phobia Society of America
5820 Hubbard Drive
Rockville, MD 20852   (301) 231-9350

Recovery
802 North Dearborn Street
Chicago, IL 60610   (312) 337-5661

Self-Help Center
1600 Dodge Avenue
Evanston, IL 60201   (312) 328-0470

Temple University, Agoraphobia Program
3401 North Broad Street
Philadelphia PA 19140

USEFUL ADDRESSES

AUSTRALIA

Australian Society of Hypnosis
c/o Department of Psychiatry
Royal Melbourne Hospital
Victoria 3052

COSH (Collective of Self-Help)
12/14 Johnstone Street
Collingwood, Victoria 3066   (03) 417-6266

WISH (Western Institute of Self-Help)
55 Duncraig Road
Applecross, Western Australia 6153   (09) 346-9500

ASHOG (Association of Self-Help Organizations and Groups)
39 Darghan Street
Glebe, New South Wales   (02) 660-6136

Index

adrenalin 18, 19, 20–1, 22, 26–7
agoraphobia 127–9, 133–5
anxiety 91–2, 96–116, 136,
    145–61 *see also* phobia
  attacks 98, 108–16
  and conditioning 100–3
  definition of 96
  effects of 96–7, 98–9, 104–5,
    107, 113–16
  free-floating *see* persistent
    anxiety
  persistent 98, 104–8
  and repression 101, 106
  'self-help' treatment 106–8,
    110–16
  self-hypnosis for 107–8
  social anxiety 96–7, 120–2,
    145–62
  states and traits 96–100
  and stress 99–100, 105
  types of 96–100
  and worry 136–9
apprehension *see* anxiety
arousal 19, 26–7, 104–5, 111–12,
    118
autonomic nervous system
    18–19, 47, 77, 96
autosuggestion 68–70

beliefs, personal:
  as a cause of stress 35–43,
    153–9
  changing 36–40, 154–5

bonding, parent-child 85–7

conditioning 77, 101–3, 111–12,
    117–19, 146
conscious mind 16, 19, 23
  in anxiety 102–3
  in hypnosis 57–8, 66
coping behaviour 24–6, 30 *see
    also* defence mechanisms
cortex, of brain 77
corticoid hormones 20–1
counselling 37–8, 81, 94

defence mechanisms 24–6
  denial 25
  displacement 24
  intellectualisation 26
  rationalisation 25–6
  reaction formation 26
  repression 25
dependency 42, 87, 105, 158
depersonalisation 114
depression 79–95
  characteristics of 80–3
  depressive illness 80–4
  frequency of 79
  manic-depressive illness 80
  reactive depression 84–95
  self-hypnosis for 94
  treatment for 84, 94–5
  types of 79–83
derealisation 114
desensitisation 129–33, 134–5

INDEX

emotional problems:
  frequency of 75
  see individual emotions, e.g.
    depression
emotional stability 76–8
emotionality 136
expectations 86, 150–1
extroversion 76–8

failure, fear of 147–8, 158
fears and phobias 97–8, 117–35
'fight or flight' response 18–19

generalisation 102, 119, 122

heart disease 27–8
  and personality 28
hypertension 19–20, 22
hypnosis 57–9 *see also*
  self-hypnosis

ideal self 148–9
implosion 135
inferiority, feelings of 151–2, 157–8
intellectualisation 26
introversion 76–8, 86

learned helplessness 87–8
loss events 85–6

'nervous tension' *see* tension *and* anxiety
neurosis 74–8
  definition of 74
  and personality 75–6

palliation behaviour *see* coping behaviour
palpitations 114–15
panic, feelings of 98, 105, 114–15
parasympathetic nervous system 18, 47, 115

personality 75–8
  and heart disease 28
  and neurosis 76
phobia 97–8, 117–35
  agoraphobia 127–9, 133–5
  and conditioning 117–19
  definition of 117
  desensitisation 129–33
  illness phobias 125–7
  origins of 117–29
  and repression 122–5
  'self-help' treatment 129–35
  'social phobia' 120–2
  and worry 124
positive thinking 142–4
psychosis 75

rationalisation 25–6
reactive depression 84–95
  and anxiety 91–2
  causes of 85–91
  self-hypnosis for 94–5
rejection, fear of 147–8, 158
relaxation 47–56, 111–13
  benefits of 47, 53–4, 56
  methods of 48–54
  'rapid relaxation' 54–6
repression 25, 71–2, 88, 100–1, 122–4

self-confidence 152
  improving 161–2
self-esteem 148–50, 156–7
self-hypnosis 57–73 *see also*
  autosuggestion, tape recorder technique, visualisation
  for anxiety 107–8
  for confidence 162
  for depression 94–5
  for relaxation 64
  for worried thinking 141–2
  induction script 61–4
self-talk 137–9, 142–4

shyness 145 *see also* social anxiety
social anxiety 145–62
  causes of 145–52
Social Readjustment Rating Scale (SRRS) 32–4
social skills 161–2
startle response 111
stress 15–46, 153–5
  and anxiety 99–100
  benefits of 26–7
  coping behaviour and 23–6
  definition of 15
  and depression 88–91
  effects of 17, 19–23, 27–9, 30–4
  employment-related 27–9, 38–40
  and home life 19, 23, 31, 36–7, 88–91, 105–6, 109
  mechanism of 18–9, 20–1
  personal beliefs and 35–43, 153–9
  recognising stress 30–4
  reducing stress 43–6
subconscious mind 16, 19, 23
  and anxiety 102–3
  and hypnosis 57–8
  and phobias 122–3, 124

tape recorder technique 59–68, 71–3 *see also* self-hypnosis
tension 19, 35, 48–52, 114, 115 *see also* emotional problems
tranquillisers 24, 35, 81

ulcer, stomach 20, 22

visualisation 70, 131–2, 159–60 *see also* self-hypnosis

Weekes, Claire 112, 113, 128
worried thinking 99, 121, 124–6, 136–44
worry *see* worried thinking